Maya

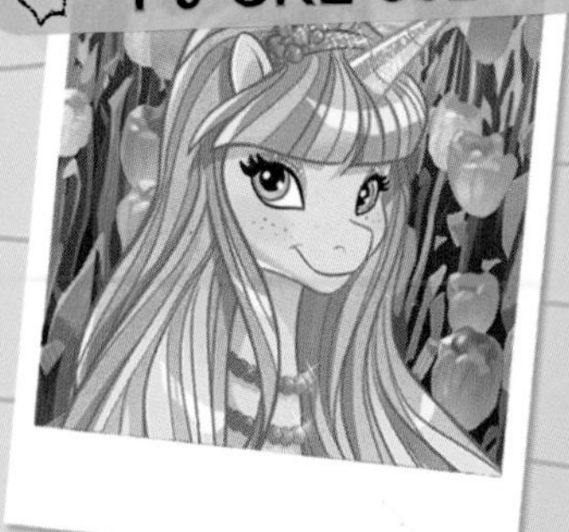

Her realm: Spring

Her personality: shy and sweet

Her passion: cooking

Her gift: the Power of Heat

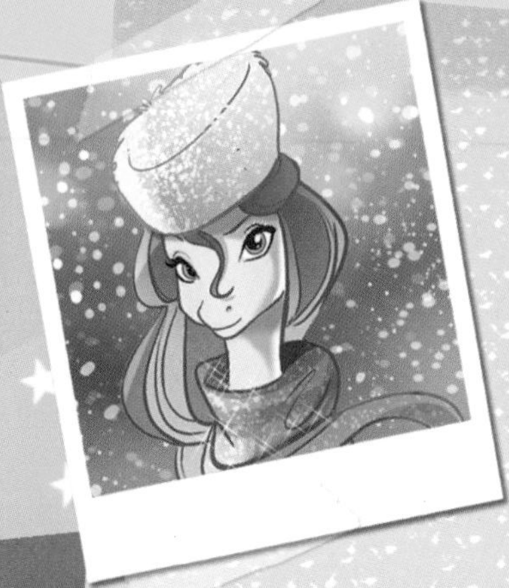

Cora

Her realm: Winter

Her personality: proud and sincere

Her passion: ice-skating

Her gift: the Power of Cold

Selena

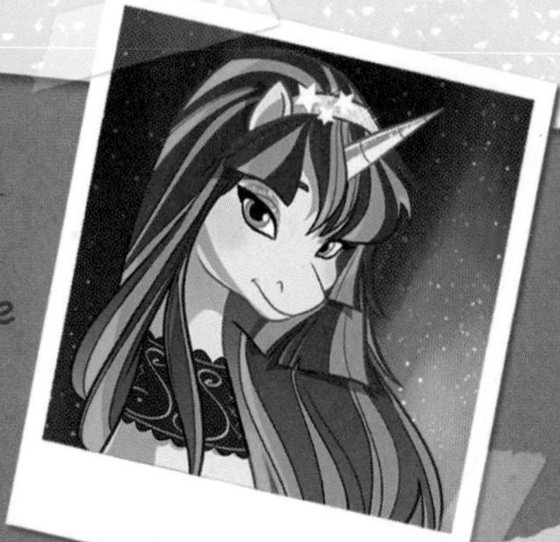

Her realm: Night

Her personality: deep and sensitive

Her passion: music

Her gift: the Power of Darkness

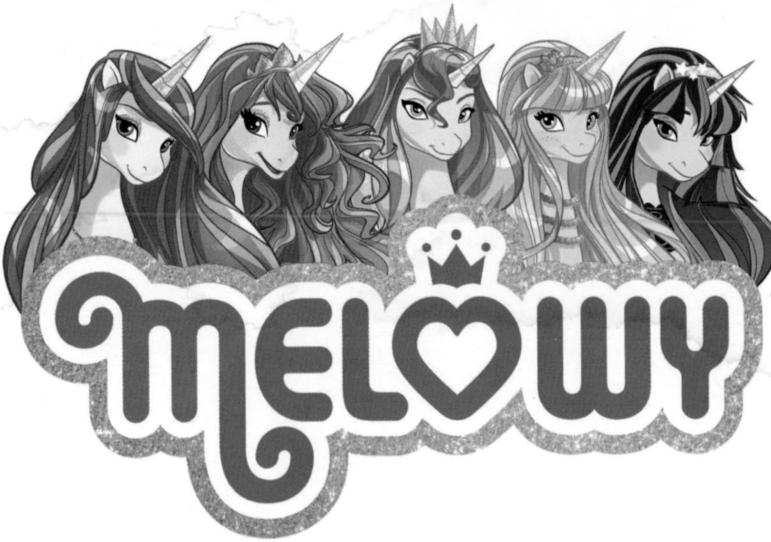
MELOWY

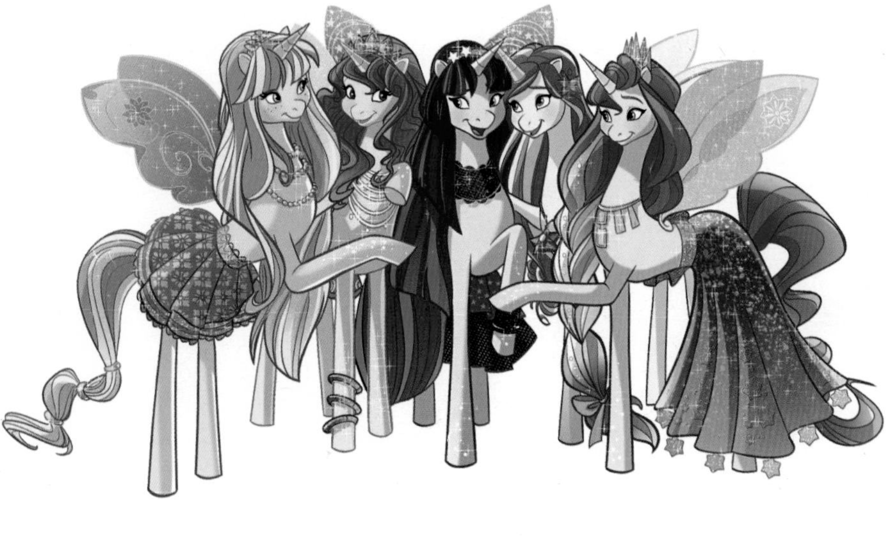

PAPERCUTZ

MORE GREAT GRAPHIC NOVEL SERIES AVAILABLE FROM PAPERCUT

THE SMURFS #21 — THE GARFIELD SHOW #6 — BARBIE #1 — THE SISTERS #1 — TROLLS #1

GERONIMO STILTON #17 — THEA STILTON #6 — SEA CREATURES #1 — THE LUNCH WITCH #1 — SCARLETT

ANNE OF GREEN BAGELS #1 — DRACULA MARRIES FRANKENSTEIN! — THE RED SHOES — THE LITTLE MERMAID — FUZZY BASEBALL

HOTEL TRANSYLVANIA #1 — THE LOUD HOUSE #1 — MANOSAURS #1 — THE ONLY LIVING BOY #5 — GUMBY #1

THE SMURFS, THE GARFIELD SHOW, BARBIE, HOTEL TRANSYLVANIA, MANOSAURS, THE LOUD HOUSE and TROLLS graphic novels are available for $7.99 in paperback, and $12.99 in hardcover. THE ONLY LIVING BOY and GUMBY graphic novels are available for $8.99 in paperback, and $13.99 hardcover. GERONIMO STILTON and THEA STILTON graphic novels are available for $9.99 in hardcover only. FUZZY BASEBALL graphic novels are available for $9.99 in paperback only. THE LUNCH WITCH, SCARLETT, and ANNE OF GREEN BAGELS graphic novels are available for $14.99 in paperback on THE RED SHOES and THE LITTLE MERMAID graphic novels are available for $12.99 in hardcover only. DRACULA MARRIES FRANKENSTEIN! graphic novels available for $12.99 in paperback only. THE SISTERS graphic novels are available for $9.99 in paperback, and $14.99 in hardcover. SEA CREATURES graphic novels are available for $10.99 in hardcover only.

Available from booksellers everywhere. You can also order online from www.papercutz.com. Or call 1-800-886-1223, Monday through Friday, 9–5 EST. M Visa, and AmEx accepted. To order by mail, please add $5.00 for postage and handling for first book ordered, $1.00 for each additional book and mak check payable to NBM Publishing. Send to: Papercutz, 160 Broadway, Suite 700, East Wing, New York, NY 10038.

THE SMURFS, GUMBY, THE GARFIELD SHOW, THE LOUD HOUSE, THE ONLY LIVING BOY, BARBIE, TROLLS, GERONIMO STILTON, THEA STILTON, FUZ BASEBALL, THE LUNCH WITCH, THE LITTLE MERMAID, HOTEL TRANSYLVANIA, MANOSAURS, THE SISTERS, SEA CREATURES ,THE RED SHOES, ANNE GREEN BAGELS, DRACULA MARRIES FRANKENSTEIN!, and SCARLETT graphic novels are also available wherever e-books are sold.

© Peyo — 2018 - Licensed through I.M.P.S. (Brussels) - www.

MEL♡WY

The Test of Magic

Cortney Powell — Writer
Ryan Jampole — Artist
MEL♡WY created by **Danielle Star**

PAPERCUTZ™
New York

MELOWY #1
"The Test of Magic"

Cover by RYAN JAMPOLE
Editorial supervision by ALESSANDRA BERELLO and LISA CAPIOTTO
(Atlantyca S.p.A.)
Script by CORTNEY POWELL
Art by RYAN JAMPOLE
Color by LAURIE E. SMITH
Lettering by WILSON RAMOS JR.

Production – DAWN GUZZO
Assistant Managing Editor – JEFF WHITMAN
JIM SALICRUP
Editor-in-Chief

ISBN 978-1-54580-002-7

Printed in India
May 2018

Papercutz books may be purchased for business or promotional use.
For information on bulk purchases, please contact Macmillan
Corporate and Premium Sales Department at (800) 221-7945 x5442.

Distributed by Macmillan
First Printing

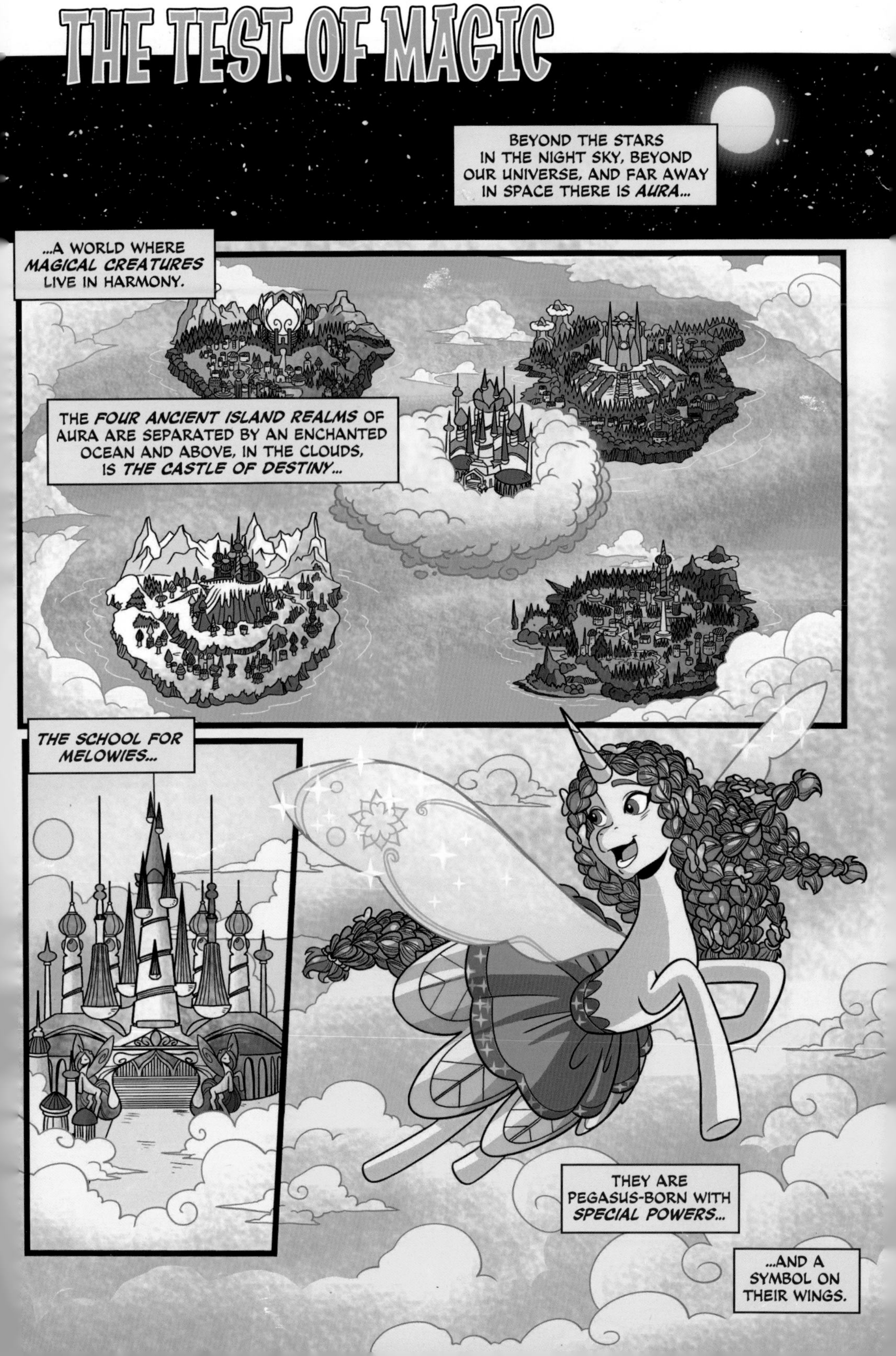
THE TEST OF MAGIC
BEYOND THE STARS IN THE NIGHT SKY, BEYOND OUR UNIVERSE, AND FAR AWAY IN SPACE THERE IS *AURA*...
...A WORLD WHERE *MAGICAL CREATURES* LIVE IN HARMONY.
THE *FOUR ANCIENT ISLAND REALMS* OF AURA ARE SEPARATED BY AN ENCHANTED OCEAN AND ABOVE, IN THE CLOUDS, IS *THE CASTLE OF DESTINY*...
THE SCHOOL FOR MELOWIES...
THEY ARE PEGASUS-BORN WITH *SPECIAL POWERS*...
...AND A SYMBOL ON THEIR WINGS.

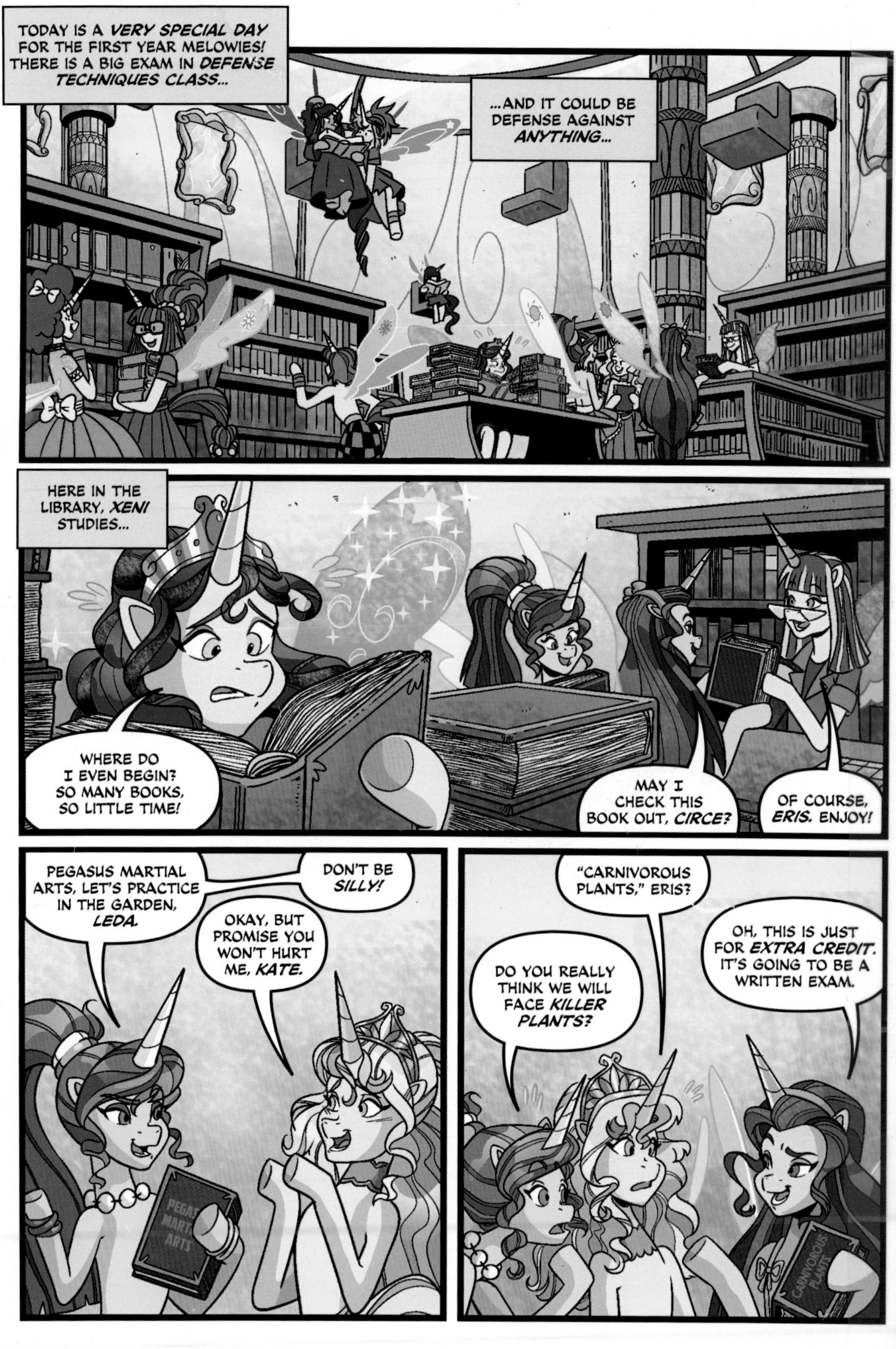
TODAY IS A VERY SPECIAL DAY FOR THE FIRST YEAR MELOWIES! THERE IS A BIG EXAM IN DEFENSE TECHNIQUES CLASS...
...AND IT COULD BE DEFENSE AGAINST ANYTHING...
HERE IN THE LIBRARY, XENI STUDIES...
WHERE DO I EVEN BEGIN? SO MANY BOOKS, SO LITTLE TIME!
MAY I CHECK THIS BOOK OUT, CIRCE?
OF COURSE, ERIS. ENJOY!
PEGASUS MARTIAL ARTS, LET'S PRACTICE IN THE GARDEN, LEDA.
DON'T BE SILLY!
OKAY, BUT PROMISE YOU WON'T HURT ME, KATE.
PEGASUS MARTIAL ARTS
"CARNIVOROUS PLANTS," ERIS?
DO YOU REALLY THINK WE WILL FACE KILLER PLANTS?
OH, THIS IS JUST FOR EXTRA CREDIT. IT'S GOING TO BE A WRITTEN EXAM.
CARNIVOROUS PLANTS

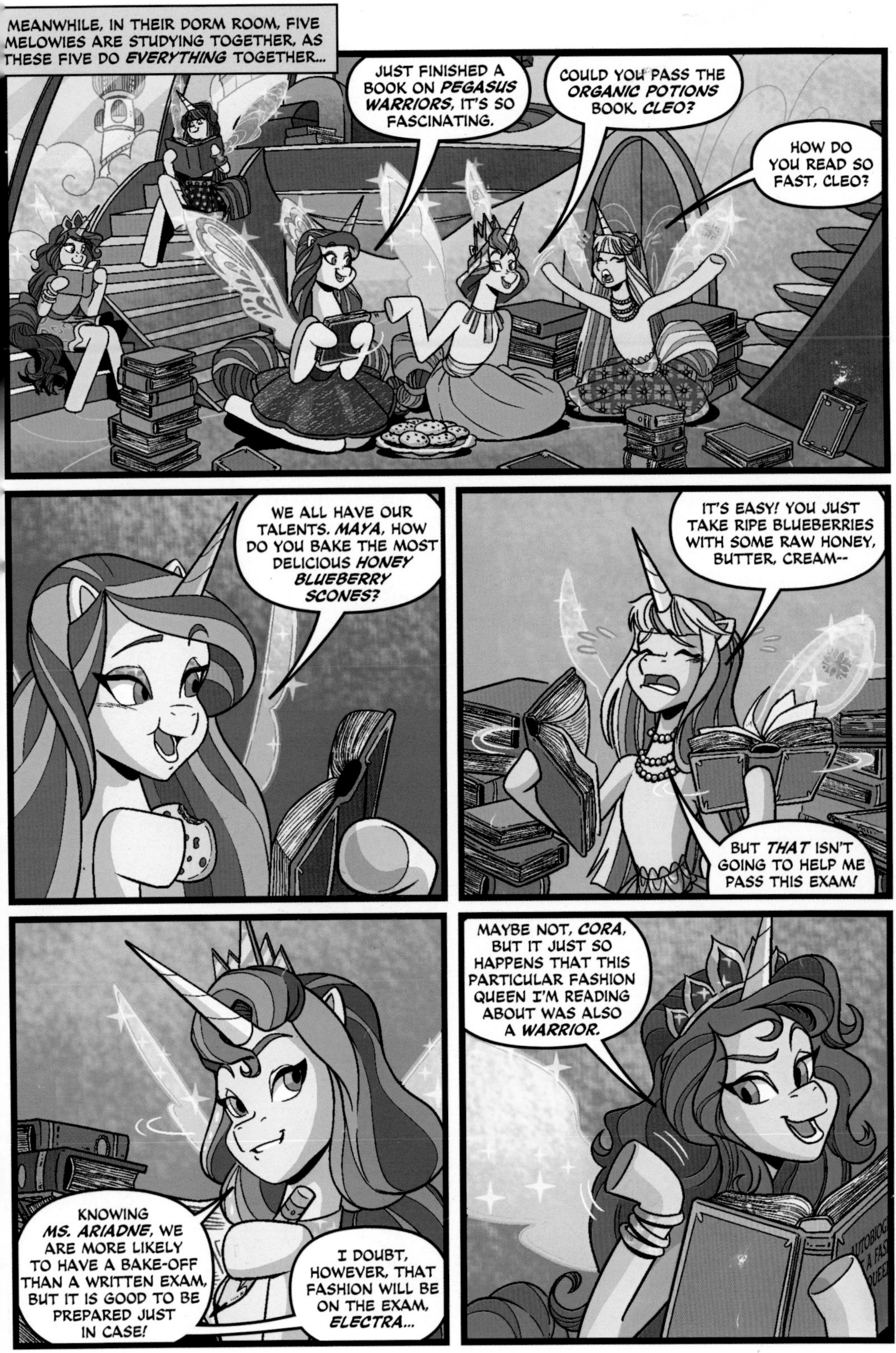
MEANWHILE, IN THEIR DORM ROOM, FIVE MELOWIES ARE STUDYING TOGETHER, AS THESE FIVE DO *EVERYTHING* TOGETHER...
JUST FINISHED A BOOK ON *PEGASUS WARRIORS*, IT'S SO FASCINATING.
COULD YOU PASS THE *ORGANIC POTIONS* BOOK, *CLEO?*
HOW DO YOU READ SO FAST, CLEO?
WE ALL HAVE OUR TALENTS. *MAYA*, HOW DO YOU BAKE THE MOST DELICIOUS *HONEY BLUEBERRY SCONES?*
IT'S EASY! YOU JUST TAKE RIPE BLUEBERRIES WITH SOME RAW HONEY, BUTTER, CREAM--
BUT *THAT* ISN'T GOING TO HELP ME PASS THIS EXAM!
KNOWING *MS. ARIADNE*, WE ARE MORE LIKELY TO HAVE A BAKE-OFF THAN A WRITTEN EXAM, BUT IT IS GOOD TO BE PREPARED JUST IN CASE!
I DOUBT, HOWEVER, THAT FASHION WILL BE ON THE EXAM, *ELECTRA*...
MAYBE NOT, *CORA*, BUT IT JUST SO HAPPENS THAT THIS PARTICULAR FASHION QUEEN I'M READING ABOUT WAS ALSO A *WARRIOR*.

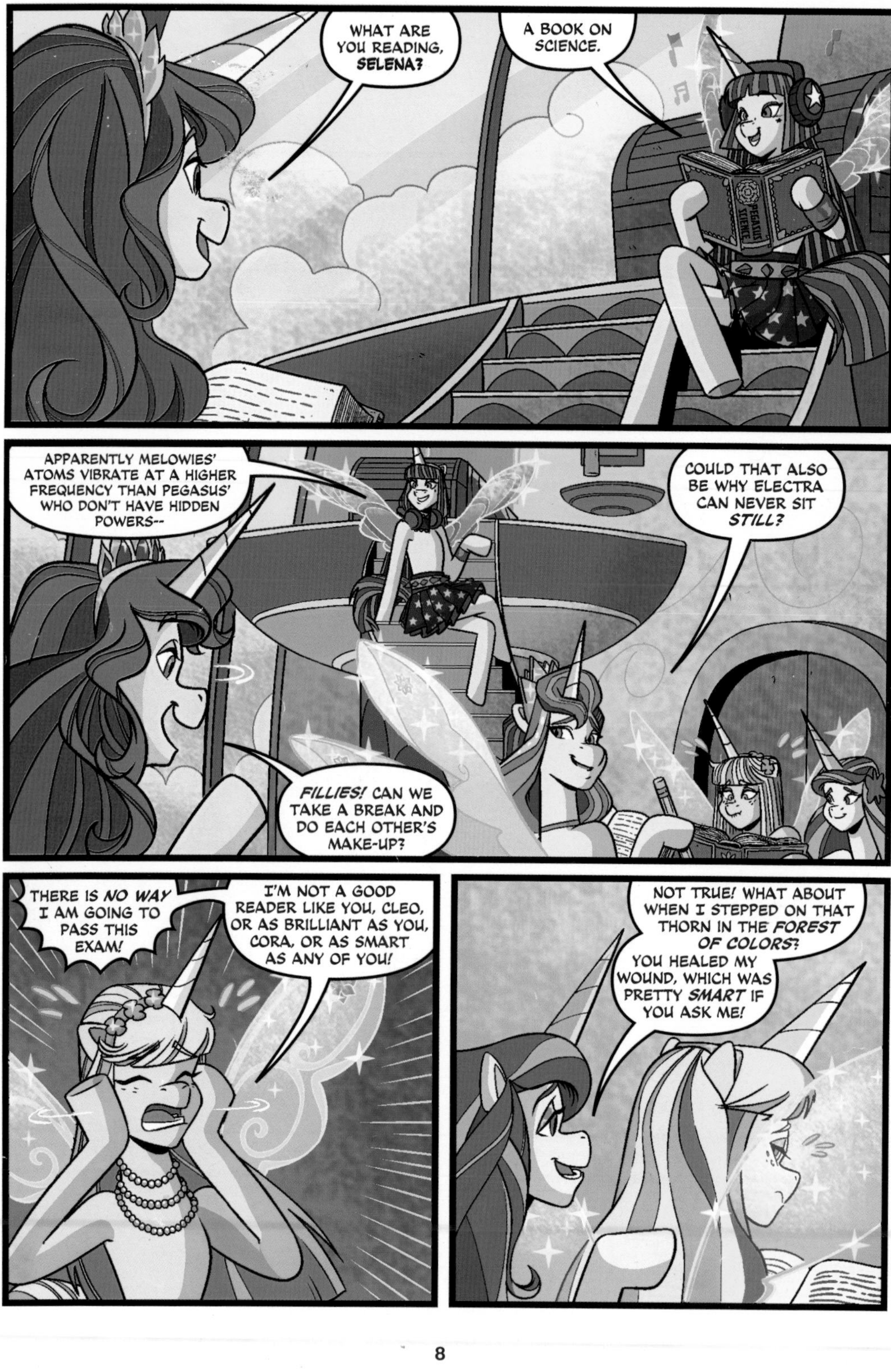
WHAT ARE YOU READING, SELENA?
A BOOK ON SCIENCE.
PEGASUS SCIENCE
APPARENTLY MELOWIES' ATOMS VIBRATE AT A HIGHER FREQUENCY THAN PEGASUS' WHO DON'T HAVE HIDDEN POWERS--
COULD THAT ALSO BE WHY ELECTRA CAN NEVER SIT STILL?
FILLIES! CAN WE TAKE A BREAK AND DO EACH OTHER'S MAKE-UP?
THERE IS NO WAY I AM GOING TO PASS THIS EXAM!
I'M NOT A GOOD READER LIKE YOU, CLEO, OR AS BRILLIANT AS YOU, CORA, OR AS SMART AS ANY OF YOU!
NOT TRUE! WHAT ABOUT WHEN I STEPPED ON THAT THORN IN THE FOREST OF COLORS?
YOU HEALED MY WOUND, WHICH WAS PRETTY SMART IF YOU ASK ME!

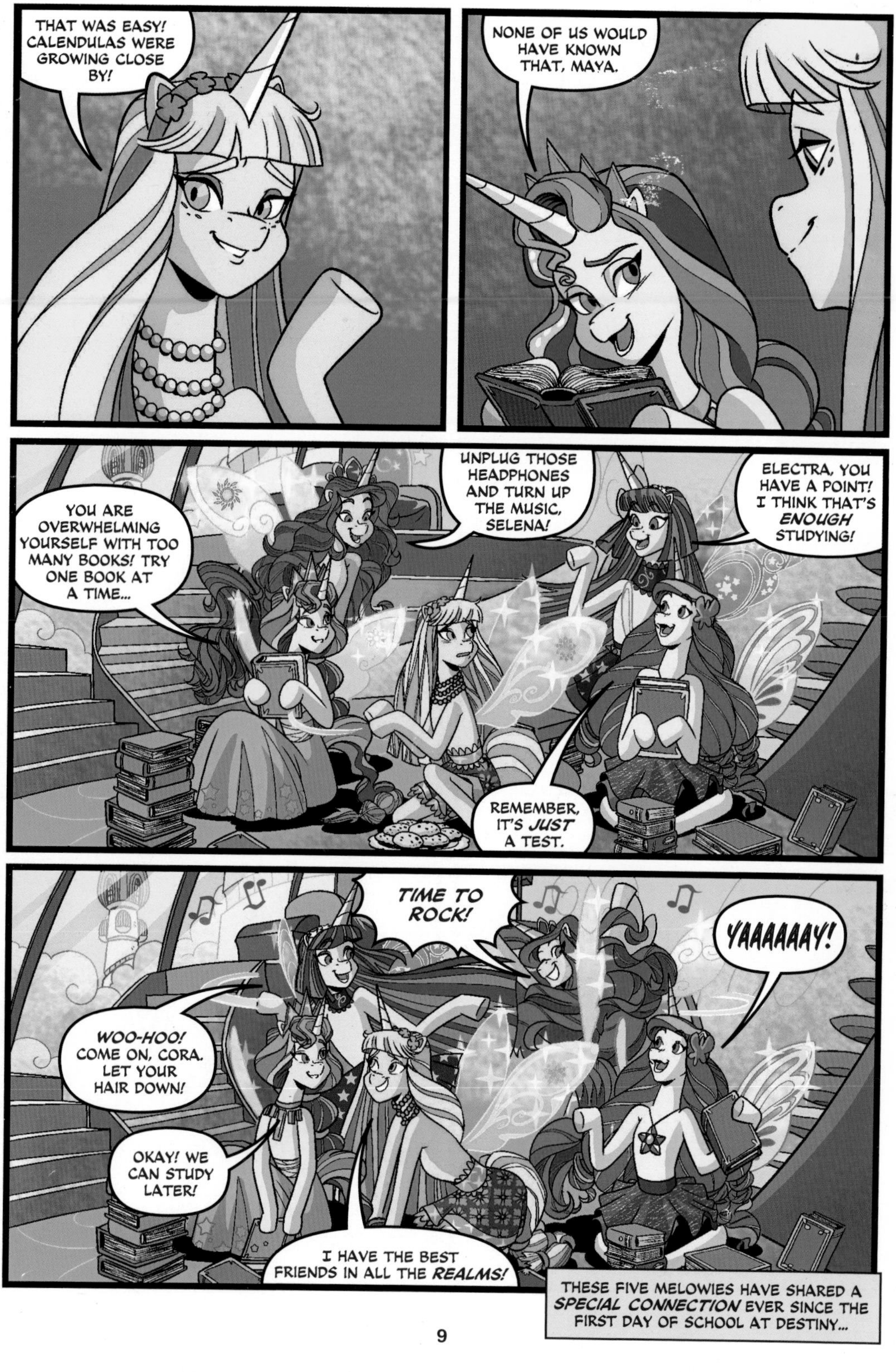
THAT WAS EASY! CALENDULAS WERE GROWING CLOSE BY!
NONE OF US WOULD HAVE KNOWN THAT, MAYA.
YOU ARE OVERWHELMING YOURSELF WITH TOO MANY BOOKS! TRY ONE BOOK AT A TIME...
UNPLUG THOSE HEADPHONES AND TURN UP THE MUSIC, SELENA!
ELECTRA, YOU HAVE A POINT! I THINK THAT'S *ENOUGH* STUDYING!
REMEMBER, IT'S *JUST* A TEST.
TIME TO ROCK!
YAAAAAAY!
WOO-HOO! COME ON, CORA. LET YOUR HAIR DOWN!
OKAY! WE CAN STUDY LATER!
I HAVE THE BEST FRIENDS IN ALL THE *REALMS!*
THESE FIVE MELOWIES HAVE SHARED A *SPECIAL CONNECTION* EVER SINCE THE FIRST DAY OF SCHOOL AT DESTINY...

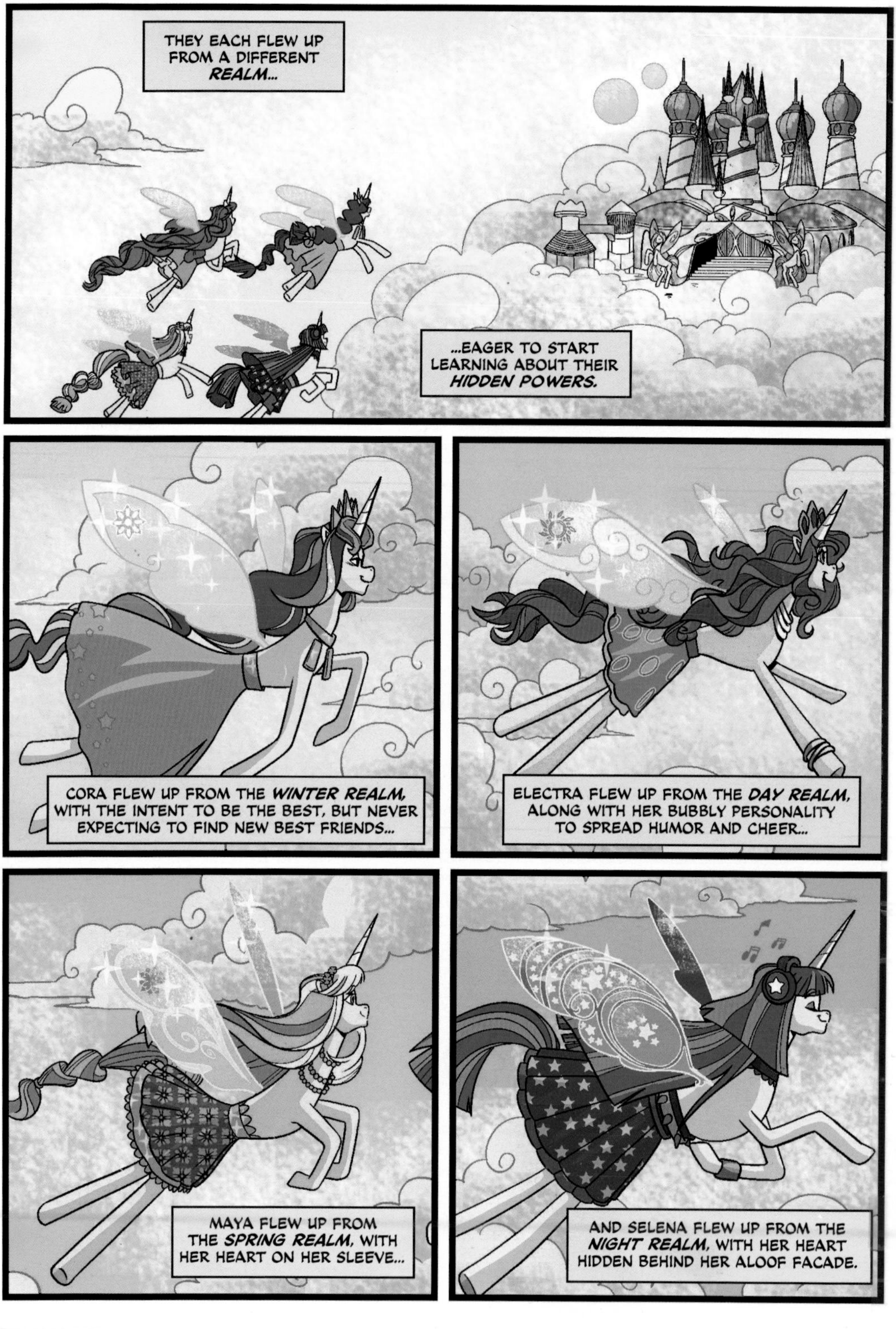
THEY EACH FLEW UP FROM A DIFFERENT *REALM*...
...EAGER TO START LEARNING ABOUT THEIR *HIDDEN POWERS.*
CORA FLEW UP FROM THE *WINTER REALM,* WITH THE INTENT TO BE THE BEST, BUT NEVER EXPECTING TO FIND NEW BEST FRIENDS...
ELECTRA FLEW UP FROM THE *DAY REALM,* ALONG WITH HER BUBBLY PERSONALITY TO SPREAD HUMOR AND CHEER...
MAYA FLEW UP FROM THE *SPRING REALM,* WITH HER HEART ON HER SLEEVE...
AND SELENA FLEW UP FROM THE *NIGHT REALM,* WITH HER HEART HIDDEN BEHIND HER ALOOF FACADE.

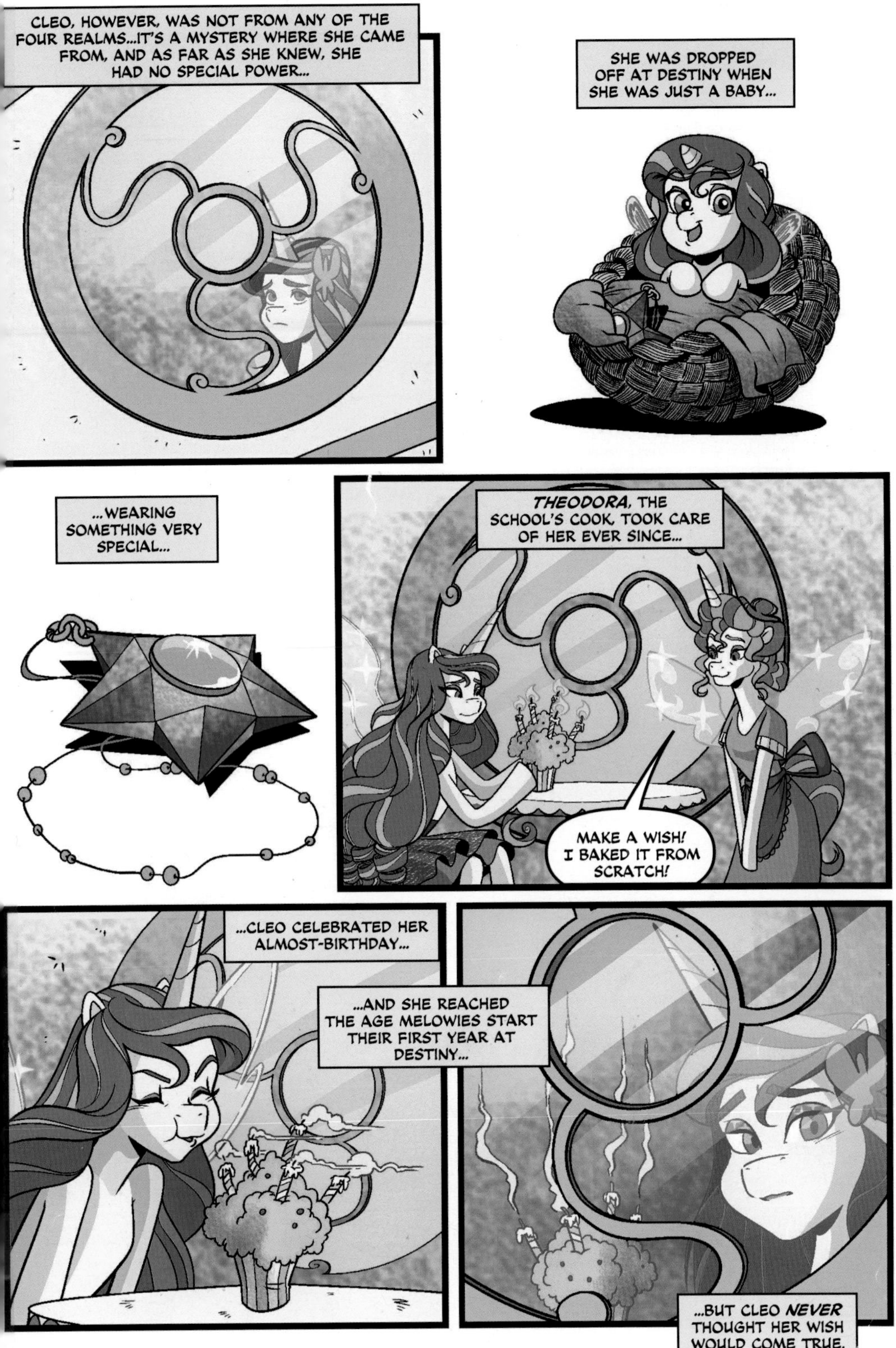
CLEO, HOWEVER, WAS NOT FROM ANY OF THE FOUR REALMS...IT'S A MYSTERY WHERE SHE CAME FROM, AND AS FAR AS SHE KNEW, SHE HAD NO SPECIAL POWER...
SHE WAS DROPPED OFF AT DESTINY WHEN SHE WAS JUST A BABY...
...WEARING SOMETHING VERY SPECIAL...
THEODORA, THE SCHOOL'S COOK, TOOK CARE OF HER EVER SINCE...
MAKE A WISH! I BAKED IT FROM SCRATCH!
...CLEO CELEBRATED HER ALMOST-BIRTHDAY...
...AND SHE REACHED THE AGE MELOWIES START THEIR FIRST YEAR AT DESTINY...
...BUT CLEO *NEVER* THOUGHT HER WISH WOULD COME TRUE.

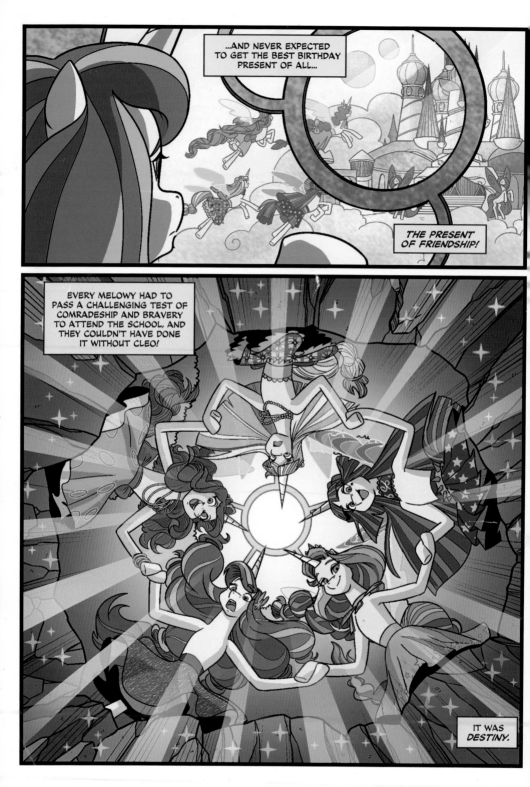

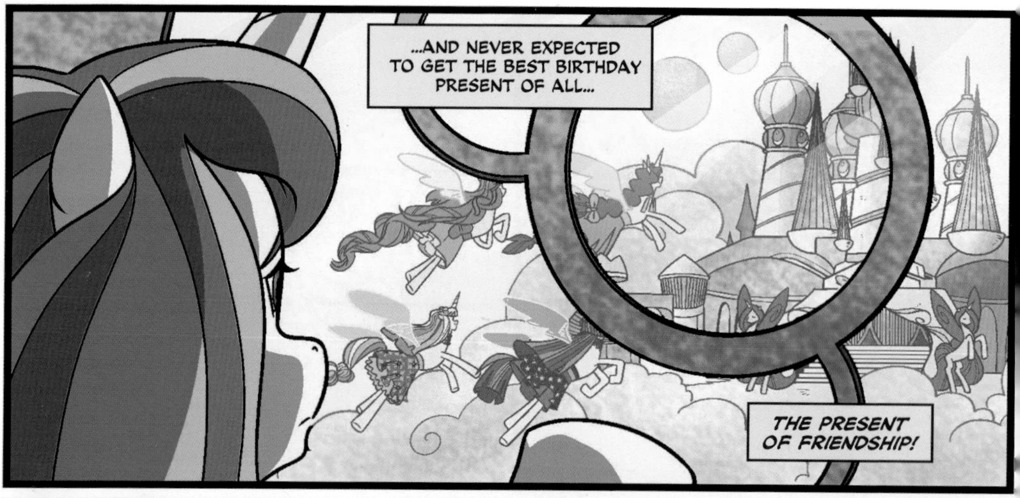
...AND NEVER EXPECTED TO GET THE BEST BIRTHDAY PRESENT OF ALL...
THE PRESENT OF FRIENDSHIP!

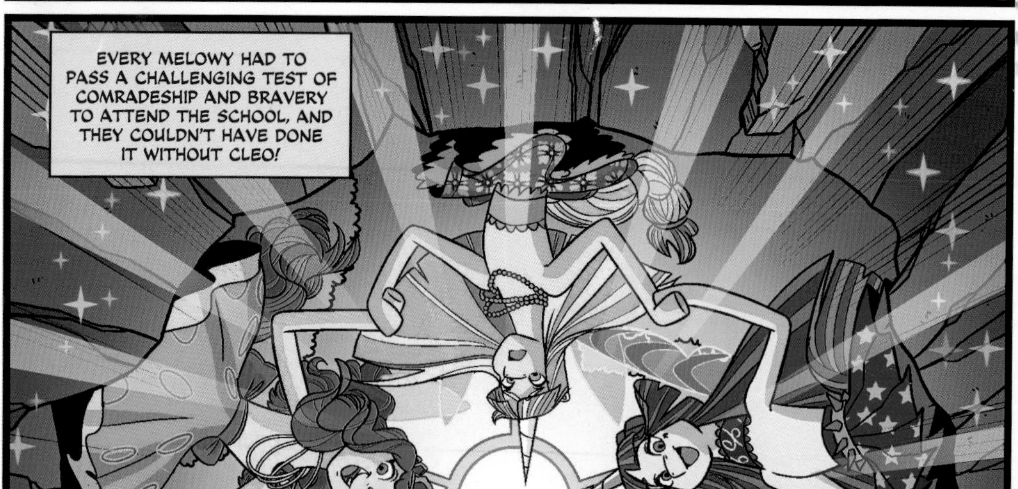
EVERY MELOWY HAD TO PASS A CHALLENGING TEST OF COMRADESHIP AND BRAVERY TO ATTEND THE SCHOOL, AND THEY COULDN'T HAVE DONE IT WITHOUT CLEO!
IT WAS DESTINY.

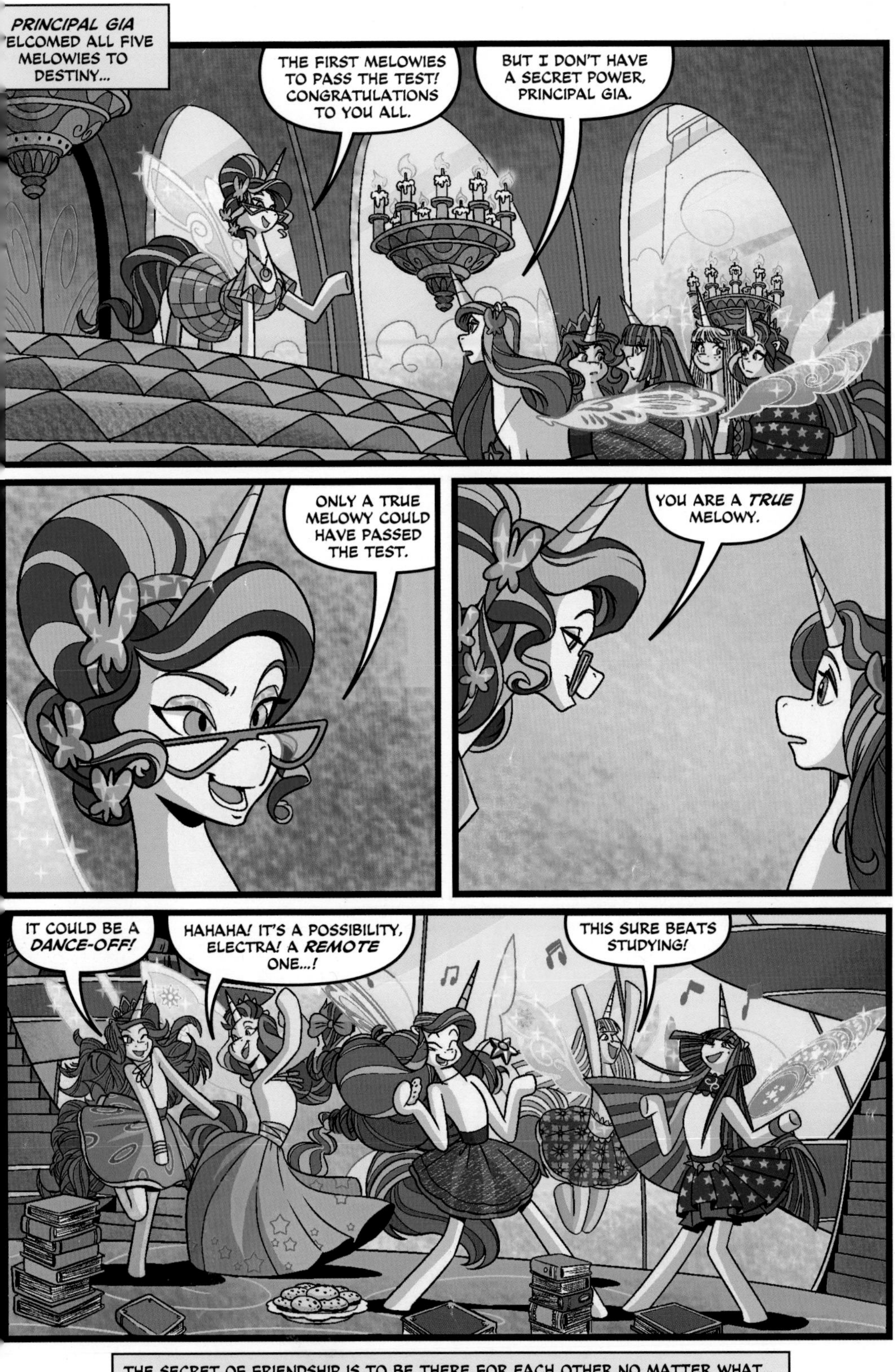
PRINCIPAL GIA ELCOMED ALL FIVE MELOWIES TO DESTINY...
THE FIRST MELOWIES TO PASS THE TEST! CONGRATULATIONS TO YOU ALL.
BUT I DON'T HAVE A SECRET POWER, PRINCIPAL GIA.
ONLY A TRUE MELOWY COULD HAVE PASSED THE TEST.
YOU ARE A TRUE MELOWY.
IT COULD BE A DANCE-OFF!
HAHAHA! IT'S A POSSIBILITY, ELECTRA! A REMOTE ONE...!
THIS SURE BEATS STUDYING!
THE SECRET OF FRIENDSHIP IS TO BE THERE FOR EACH OTHER NO MATTER WHAT... AND SOMETIMES THAT COULD MEAN DANCING TOGETHER TO RELIEVE THE STRESS OF AN UPCOMING DEFENSE TECHNIQUES EXAM...

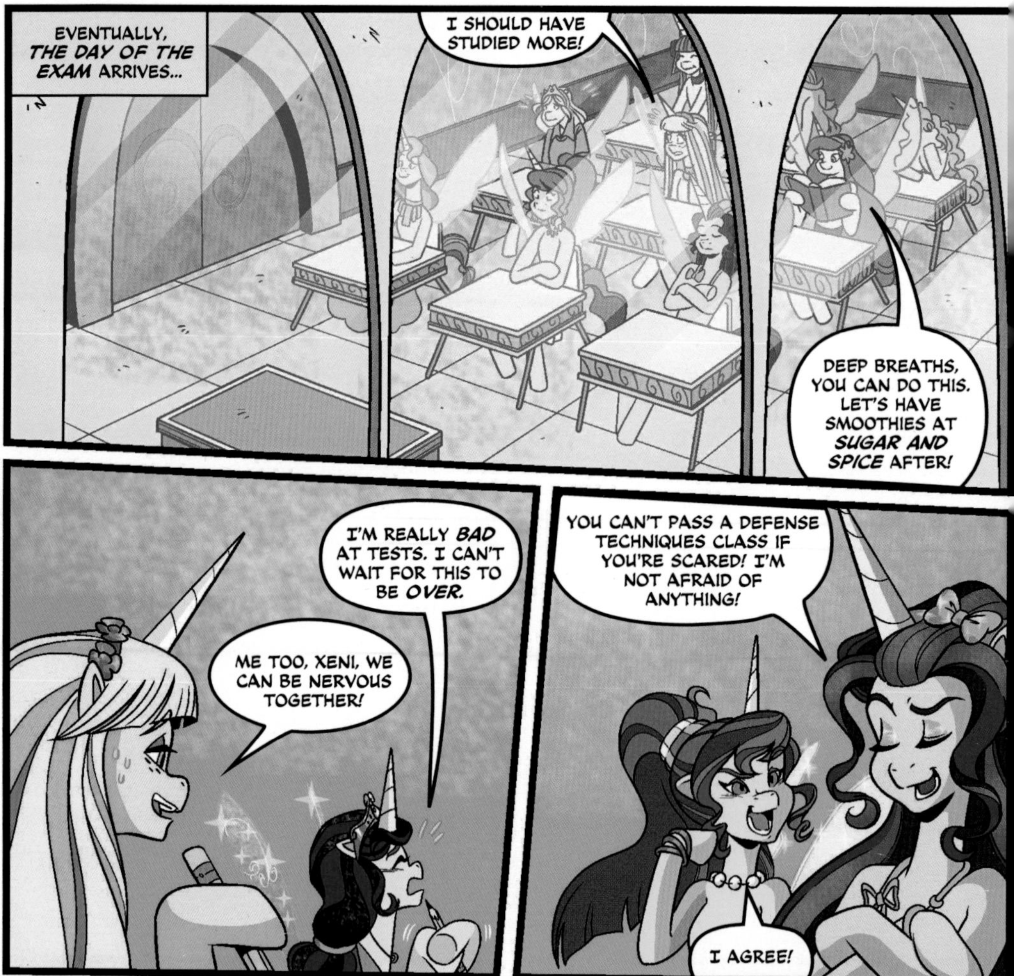
EVENTUALLY, THE DAY OF THE EXAM ARRIVES...
I SHOULD HAVE STUDIED MORE!
DEEP BREATHS, YOU CAN DO THIS. LET'S HAVE SMOOTHIES AT SUGAR AND SPICE AFTER!
I'M REALLY BAD AT TESTS. I CAN'T WAIT FOR THIS TO BE OVER.
ME TOO, XENI, WE CAN BE NERVOUS TOGETHER!
YOU CAN'T PASS A DEFENSE TECHNIQUES CLASS IF YOU'RE SCARED! I'M NOT AFRAID OF ANYTHING!
I AGREE!
BEING BRAVE AND BEING A BULLY ARE TWO DIFFERENT THINGS, ERIS.
THAT IS ENOUGH BICKERING, NORA AND PARIS!
AND PRALINE, HEADPHONES OFF!

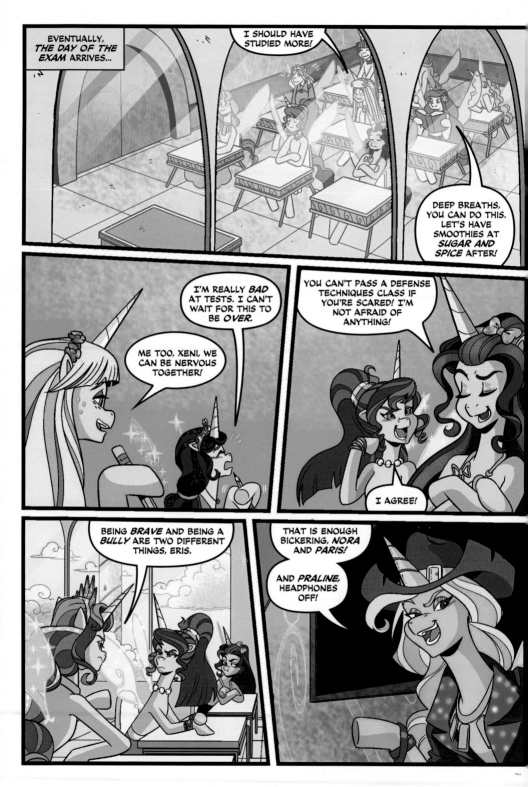

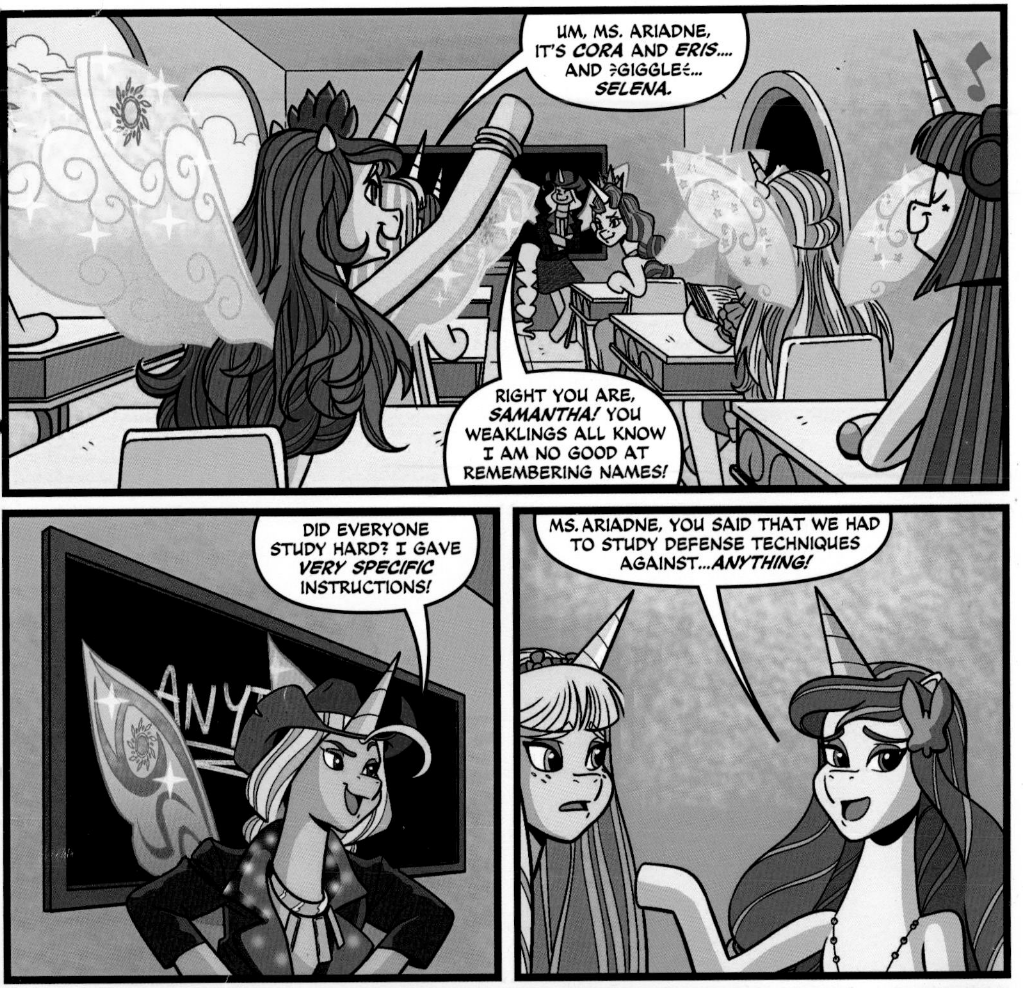
UM, MS. ARIADNE, IT'S CORA AND ERIS.... AND *GIGGLE*... SELENA.
RIGHT YOU ARE, SAMANTHA! YOU WEAKLINGS ALL KNOW I AM NO GOOD AT REMEMBERING NAMES!
DID EVERYONE STUDY HARD? I GAVE VERY SPECIFIC INSTRUCTIONS!
MS. ARIADNE, YOU SAID THAT WE HAD TO STUDY DEFENSE TECHNIQUES AGAINST...ANYTHING!
THAT'S CORRECT, RIO!
ENOUGH REVIEWING! YOU WILL ALL FOLLOW ME TO A SECRET SPOT IN THE FOREST! YOU ARE TO BE TESTED THERE!

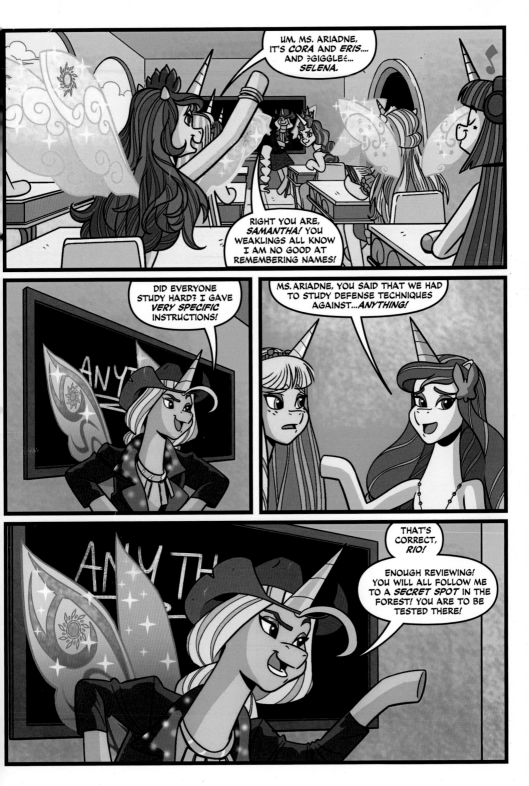

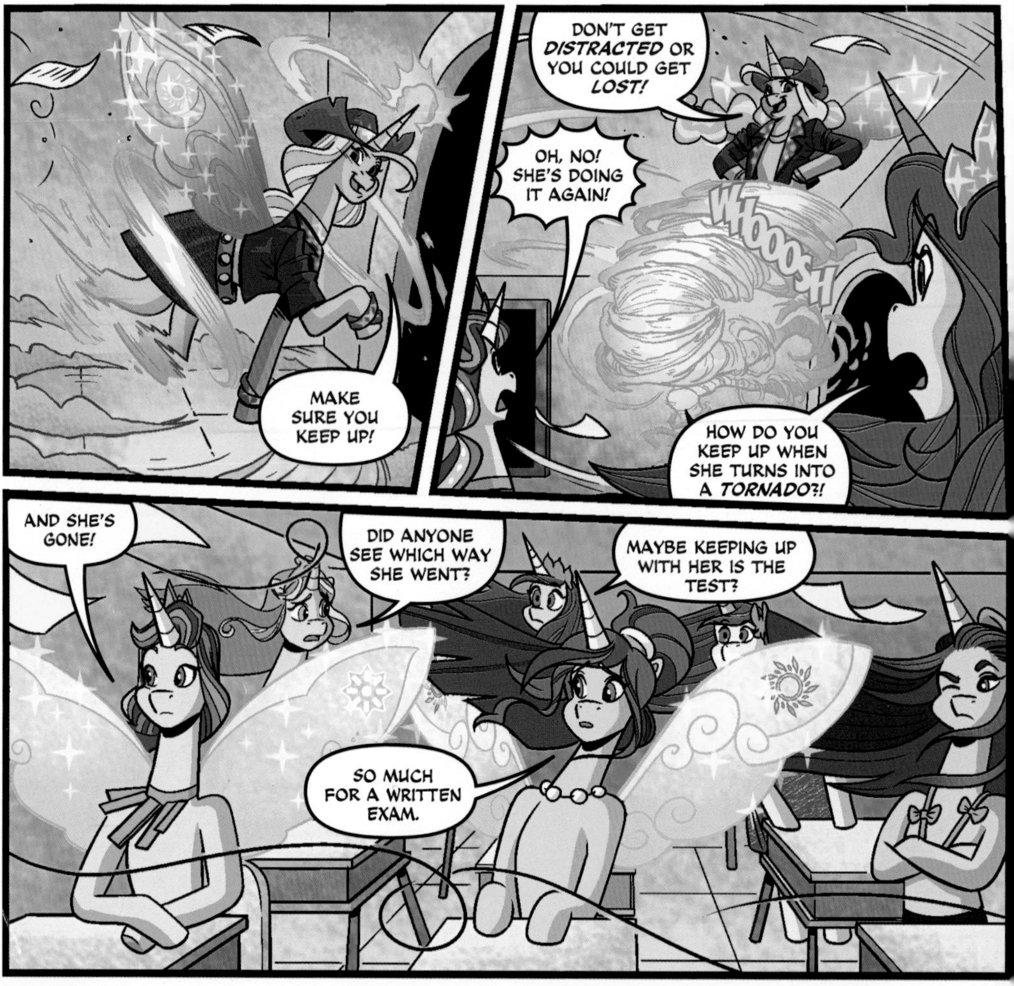
MAKE SURE YOU KEEP UP!
DON'T GET *DISTRACTED* OR YOU COULD GET *LOST!*
OH, NO! SHE'S DOING IT AGAIN!
WHOOOSH
HOW DO YOU KEEP UP WHEN SHE TURNS INTO A *TORNADO*?!
AND SHE'S GONE!
DID ANYONE SEE WHICH WAY SHE WENT?
MAYBE KEEPING UP WITH HER IS THE TEST?
SO MUCH FOR A WRITTEN EXAM.
SEE? I TOLD YOU IT WOULDN'T BE SO BAD! HAHAHA!
WHO KNEW WE WOULD HAVE TO FIND THE TEST BEFORE TAKING IT?!
WE SHOULD ALL STICK TOGETH-- *XENI*?!

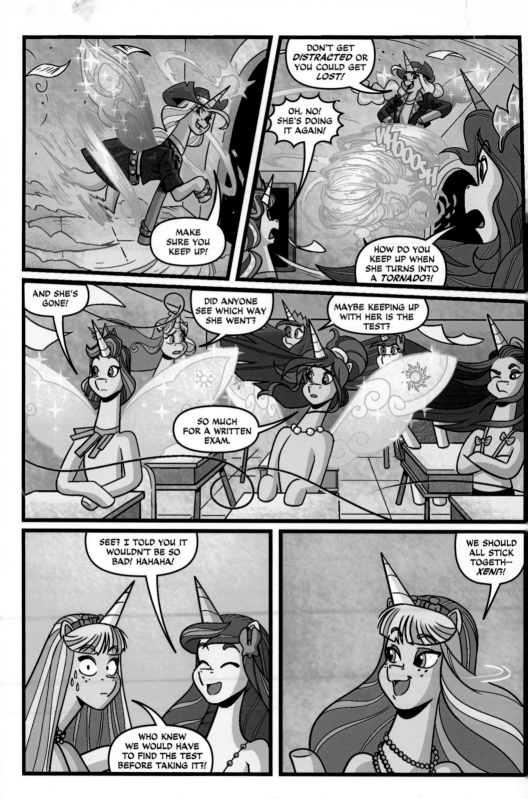

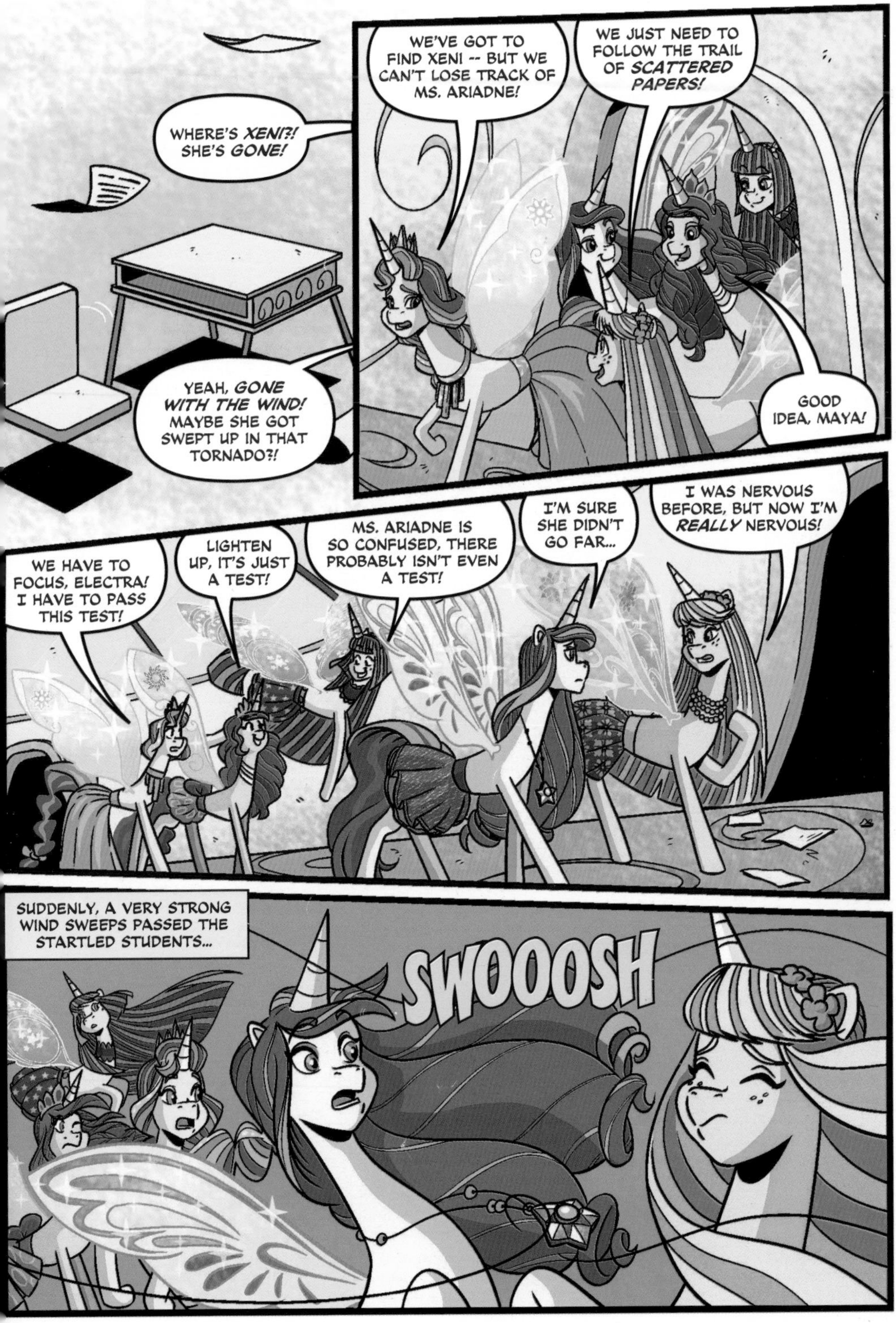
WHERE'S XENI?! SHE'S GONE!
WE'VE GOT TO FIND XENI -- BUT WE CAN'T LOSE TRACK OF MS. ARIADNE!
WE JUST NEED TO FOLLOW THE TRAIL OF SCATTERED PAPERS!
GOOD IDEA, MAYA!
YEAH, GONE WITH THE WIND! MAYBE SHE GOT SWEPT UP IN THAT TORNADO?!
WE HAVE TO FOCUS, ELECTRA! I HAVE TO PASS THIS TEST!
LIGHTEN UP, IT'S JUST A TEST!
MS. ARIADNE IS SO CONFUSED, THERE PROBABLY ISN'T EVEN A TEST!
I'M SURE SHE DIDN'T GO FAR...
I WAS NERVOUS BEFORE, BUT NOW I'M REALLY NERVOUS!
SUDDENLY, A VERY STRONG WIND SWEEPS PASSED THE STARTLED STUDENTS...
SWOOOSH

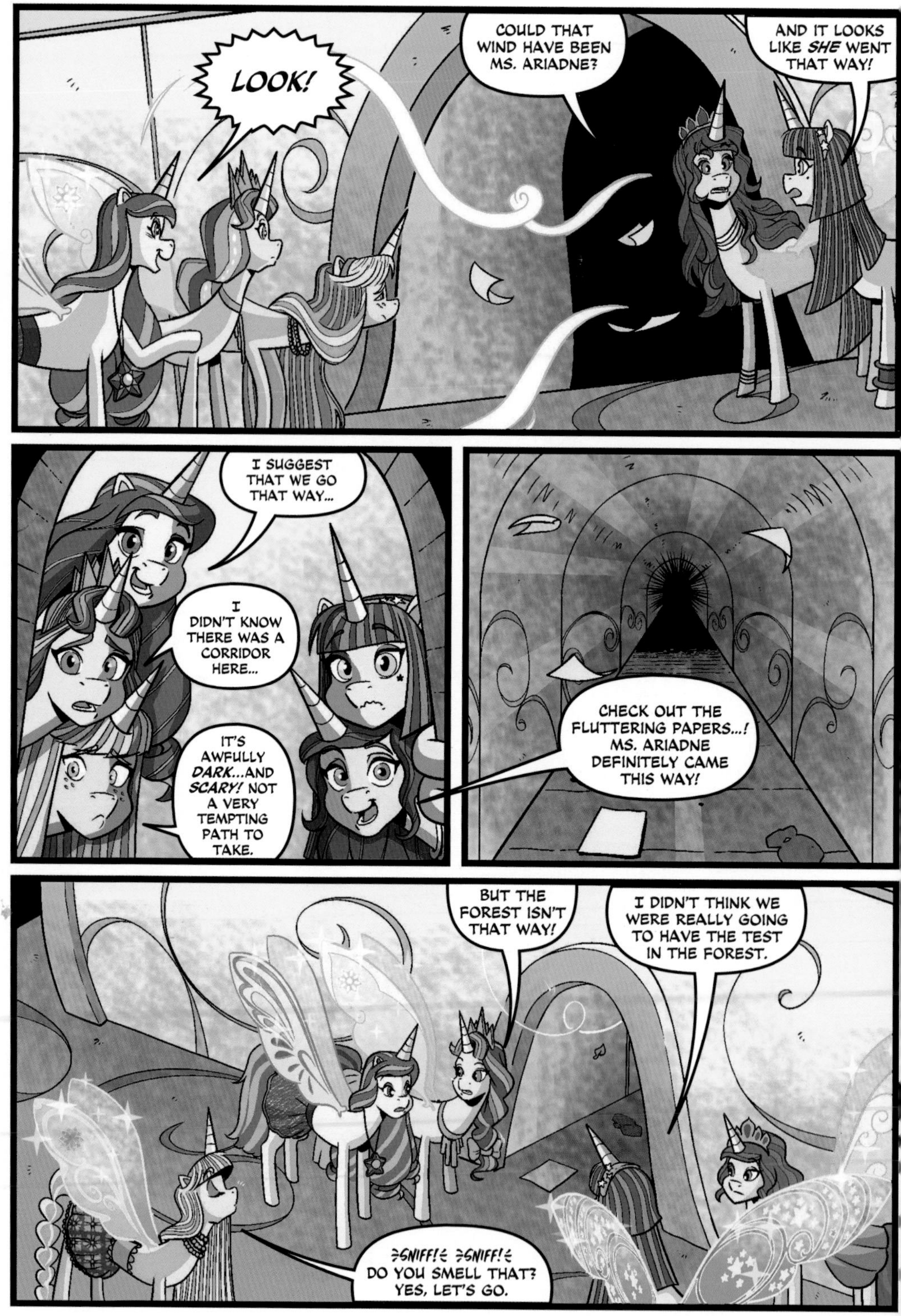
LOOK!
COULD THAT WIND HAVE BEEN MS. ARIADNE?
AND IT LOOKS LIKE SHE WENT THAT WAY!
I SUGGEST THAT WE GO THAT WAY...
I DIDN'T KNOW THERE WAS A CORRIDOR HERE...
IT'S AWFULLY DARK...AND SCARY! NOT A VERY TEMPTING PATH TO TAKE.
CHECK OUT THE FLUTTERING PAPERS...! MS. ARIADNE DEFINITELY CAME THIS WAY!
BUT THE FOREST ISN'T THAT WAY!
I DIDN'T THINK WE WERE REALLY GOING TO HAVE THE TEST IN THE FOREST.
SNIFF! SNIFF! DO YOU SMELL THAT? YES, LET'S GO.

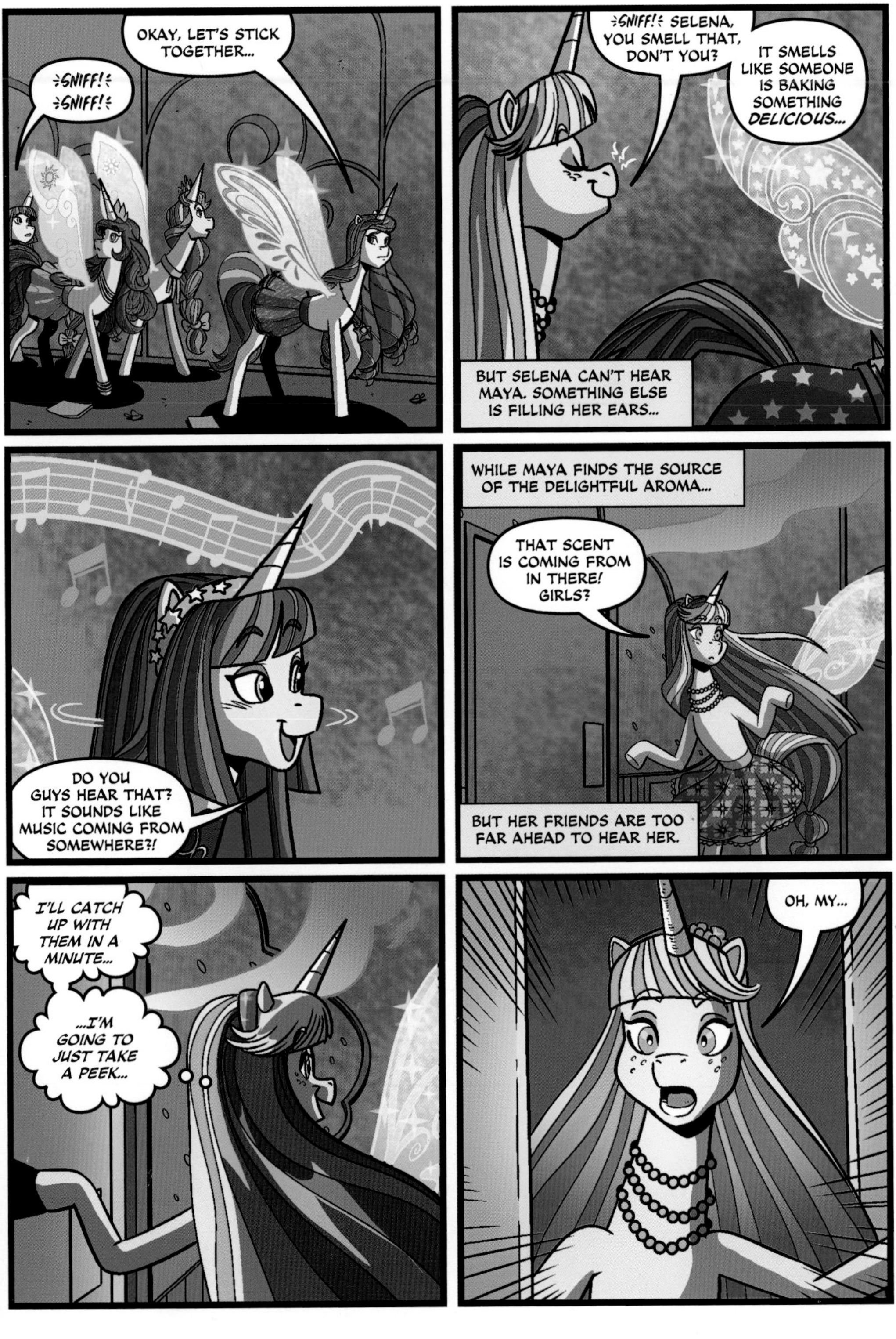

OKAY, LET'S STICK TOGETHER...
SNIFF! SNIFF!
SNIFF! SELENA, YOU SMELL THAT, DON'T YOU?
IT SMELLS LIKE SOMEONE IS BAKING SOMETHING DELICIOUS...
BUT SELENA CAN'T HEAR MAYA. SOMETHING ELSE IS FILLING HER EARS...
DO YOU GUYS HEAR THAT? IT SOUNDS LIKE MUSIC COMING FROM SOMEWHERE?!
WHILE MAYA FINDS THE SOURCE OF THE DELIGHTFUL AROMA...
THAT SCENT IS COMING FROM IN THERE! GIRLS?
BUT HER FRIENDS ARE TOO FAR AHEAD TO HEAR HER.
I'LL CATCH UP WITH THEM IN A MINUTE...
...I'M GOING TO JUST TAKE A PEEK...
OH, MY...

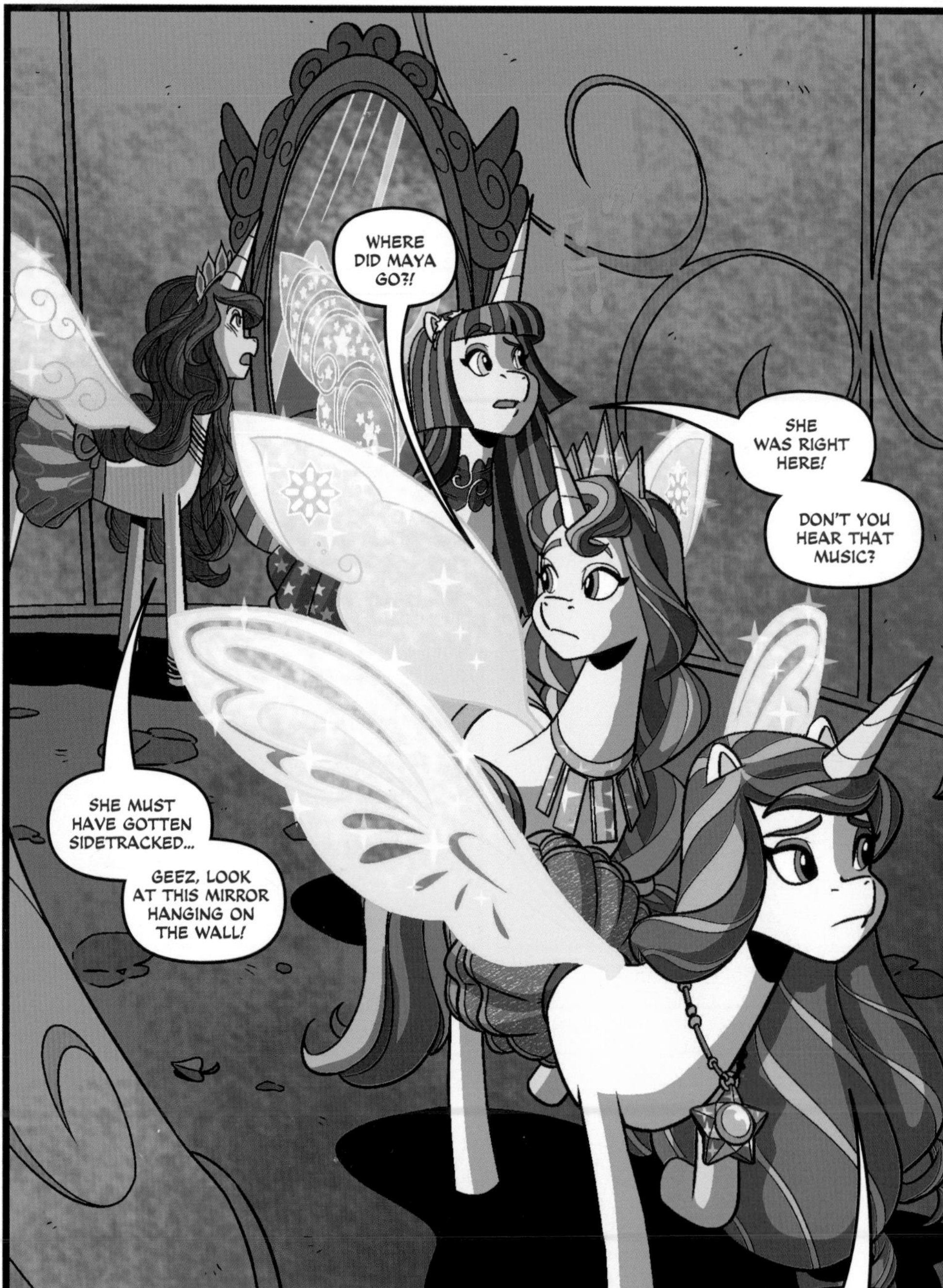
WHERE DID MAYA GO?!
SHE WAS RIGHT HERE!
DON'T YOU HEAR THAT MUSIC?
SHE MUST HAVE GOTTEN SIDETRACKED...
GEEZ, LOOK AT THIS MIRROR HANGING ON THE WALL!
SHE COULDN'T HAVE GONE FAR. LET'S GO FIND HER.

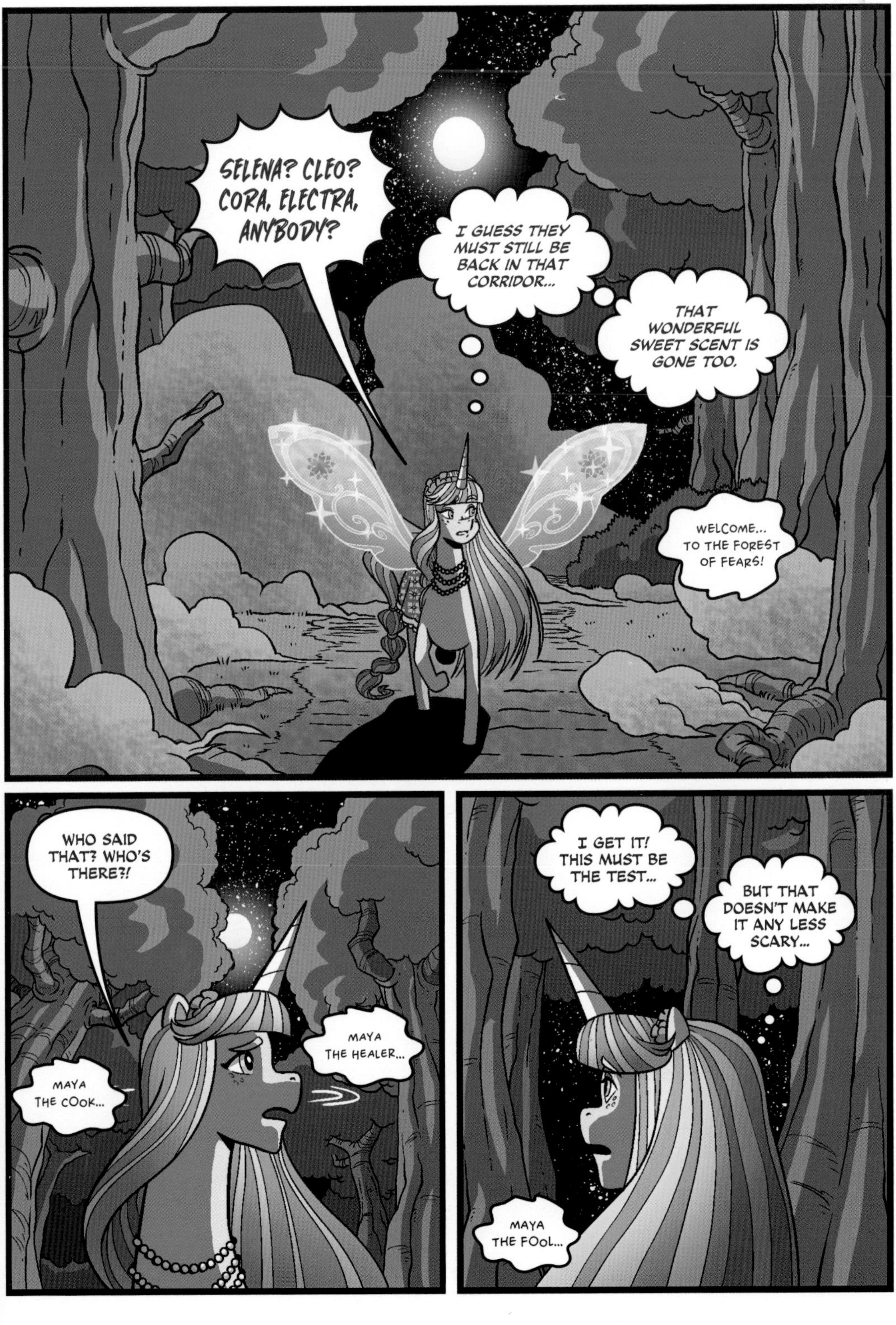
SELENA? CLEO? CORA, ELECTRA, ANYBODY?
I GUESS THEY MUST STILL BE BACK IN THAT CORRIDOR...
THAT WONDERFUL SWEET SCENT IS GONE TOO.
WELCOME... TO THE FOREST OF FEARS!
WHO SAID THAT? WHO'S THERE?!
MAYA THE HEALER...
MAYA THE COOK...
I GET IT! THIS MUST BE THE TEST...
BUT THAT DOESN'T MAKE IT ANY LESS SCARY...
MAYA THE FOOL...

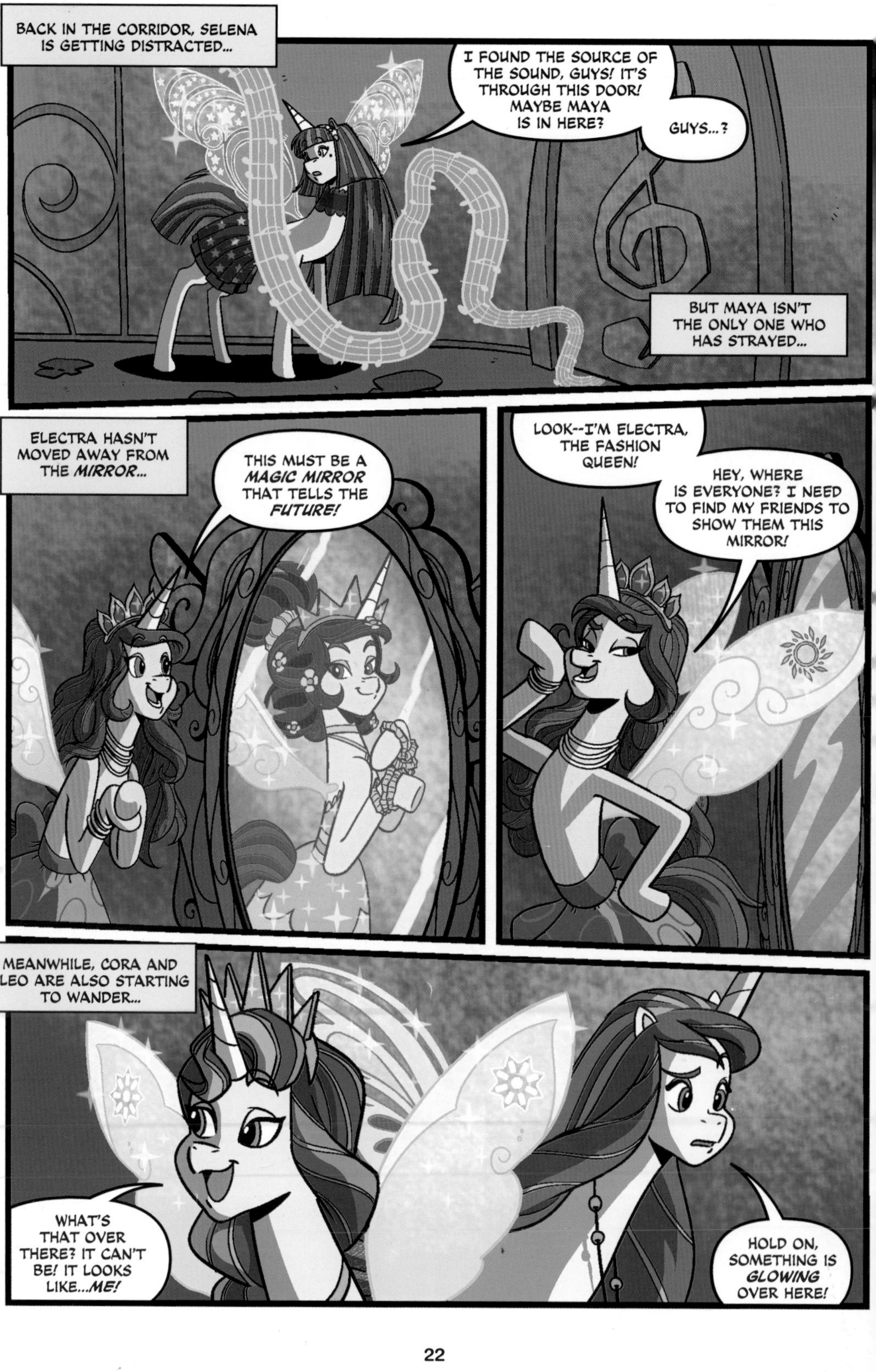
BACK IN THE CORRIDOR, SELENA IS GETTING DISTRACTED...
I FOUND THE SOURCE OF THE SOUND, GUYS! IT'S THROUGH THIS DOOR! MAYBE MAYA IS IN HERE?
GUYS...?
BUT MAYA ISN'T THE ONLY ONE WHO HAS STRAYED...
ELECTRA HASN'T MOVED AWAY FROM THE *MIRROR*...
THIS MUST BE A *MAGIC MIRROR* THAT TELLS THE *FUTURE!*
LOOK--I'M ELECTRA, THE FASHION QUEEN!
HEY, WHERE IS EVERYONE? I NEED TO FIND MY FRIENDS TO SHOW THEM THIS MIRROR!
MEANWHILE, CORA AND CLEO ARE ALSO STARTING TO WANDER...
WHAT'S THAT OVER THERE? IT CAN'T BE! IT LOOKS LIKE...*ME!*
HOLD ON, SOMETHING IS *GLOWING* OVER HERE!

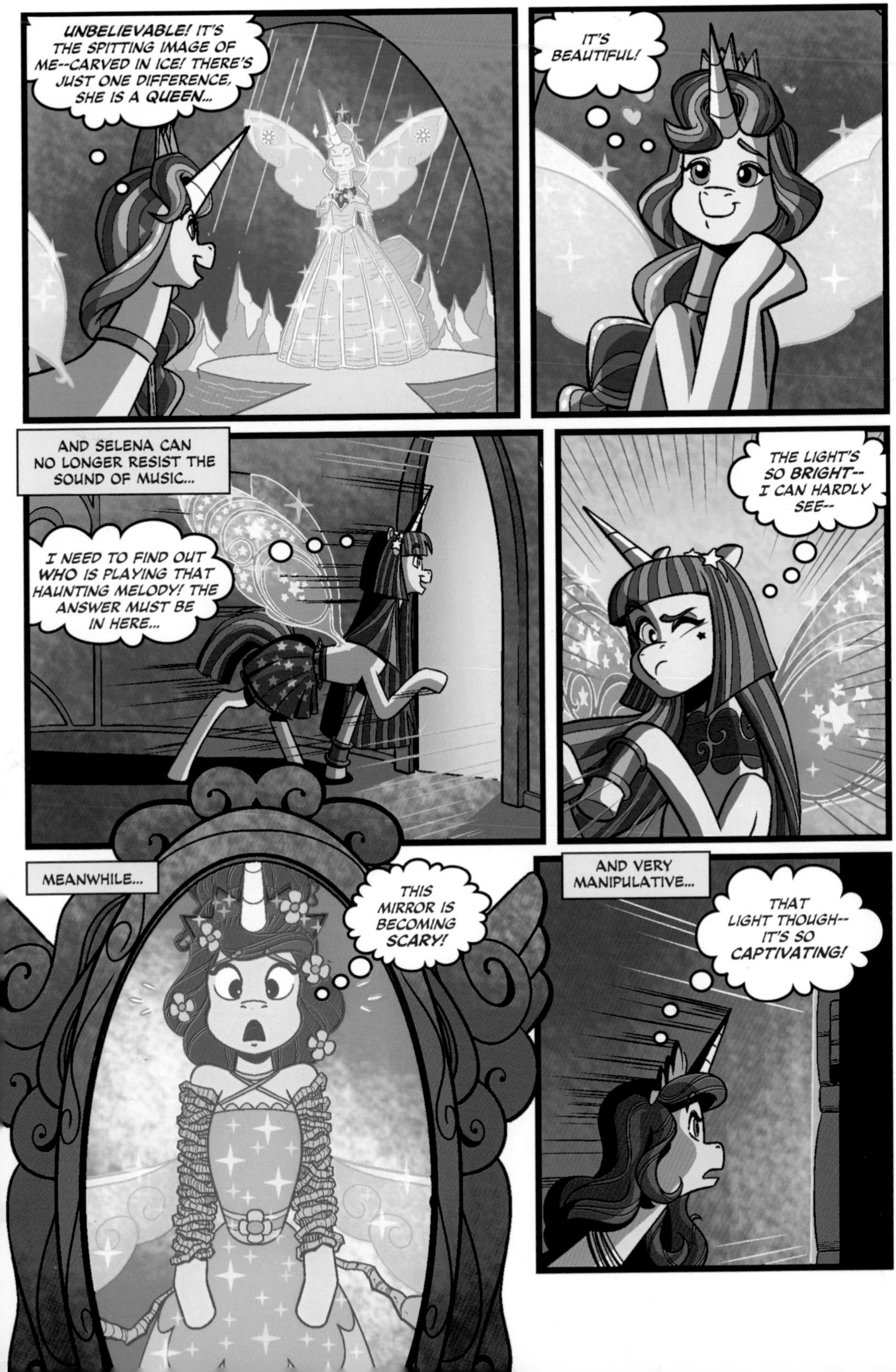
UNBELIEVABLE! IT'S THE SPITTING IMAGE OF ME--CARVED IN ICE! THERE'S JUST ONE DIFFERENCE, SHE IS A QUEEN...
IT'S BEAUTIFUL!
AND SELENA CAN NO LONGER RESIST THE SOUND OF MUSIC...
I NEED TO FIND OUT WHO IS PLAYING THAT HAUNTING MELODY! THE ANSWER MUST BE IN HERE...
THE LIGHT'S SO BRIGHT-- I CAN HARDLY SEE--
MEANWHILE...
THIS MIRROR IS BECOMING SCARY!
AND VERY MANIPULATIVE...
THAT LIGHT THOUGH-- IT'S SO CAPTIVATING!

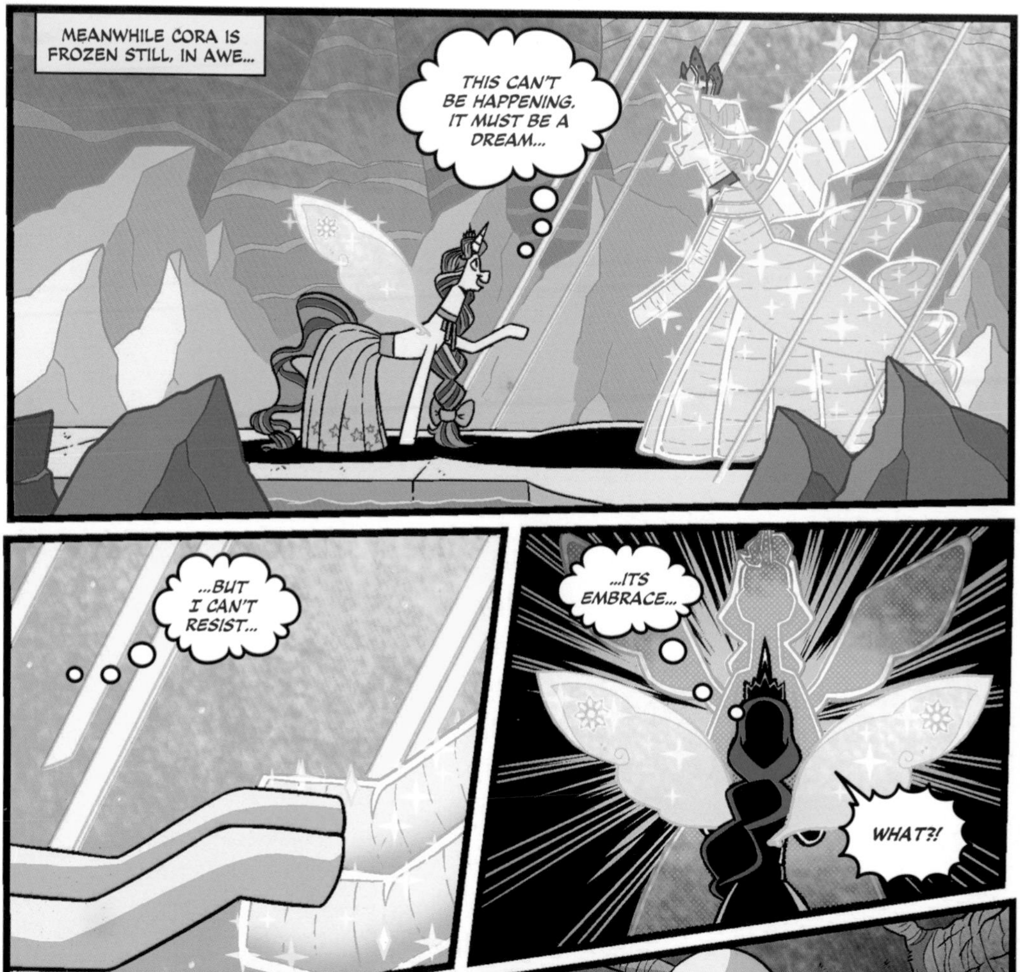
MEANWHILE CORA IS FROZEN STILL, IN AWE...
THIS CAN'T BE HAPPENING. IT MUST BE A DREAM...
...BUT I CAN'T RESIST...
...ITS EMBRACE...
WHAT?!
AND JUST LIKE THAT, THE ICE QUEEN TAKES CORA AWAY FROM HER PLEASANT DREAM AND INTO...
THE FOREST OF FEARS!
WHAT'S HAPPENING?! WHERE AM I?

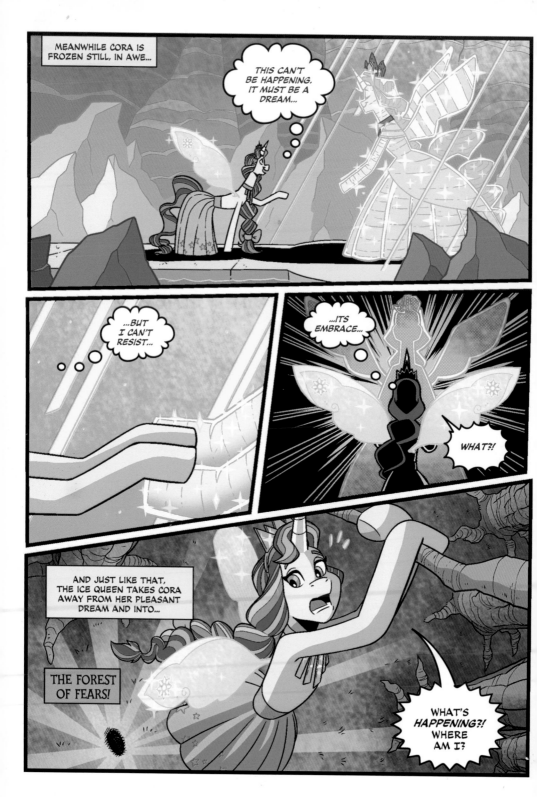

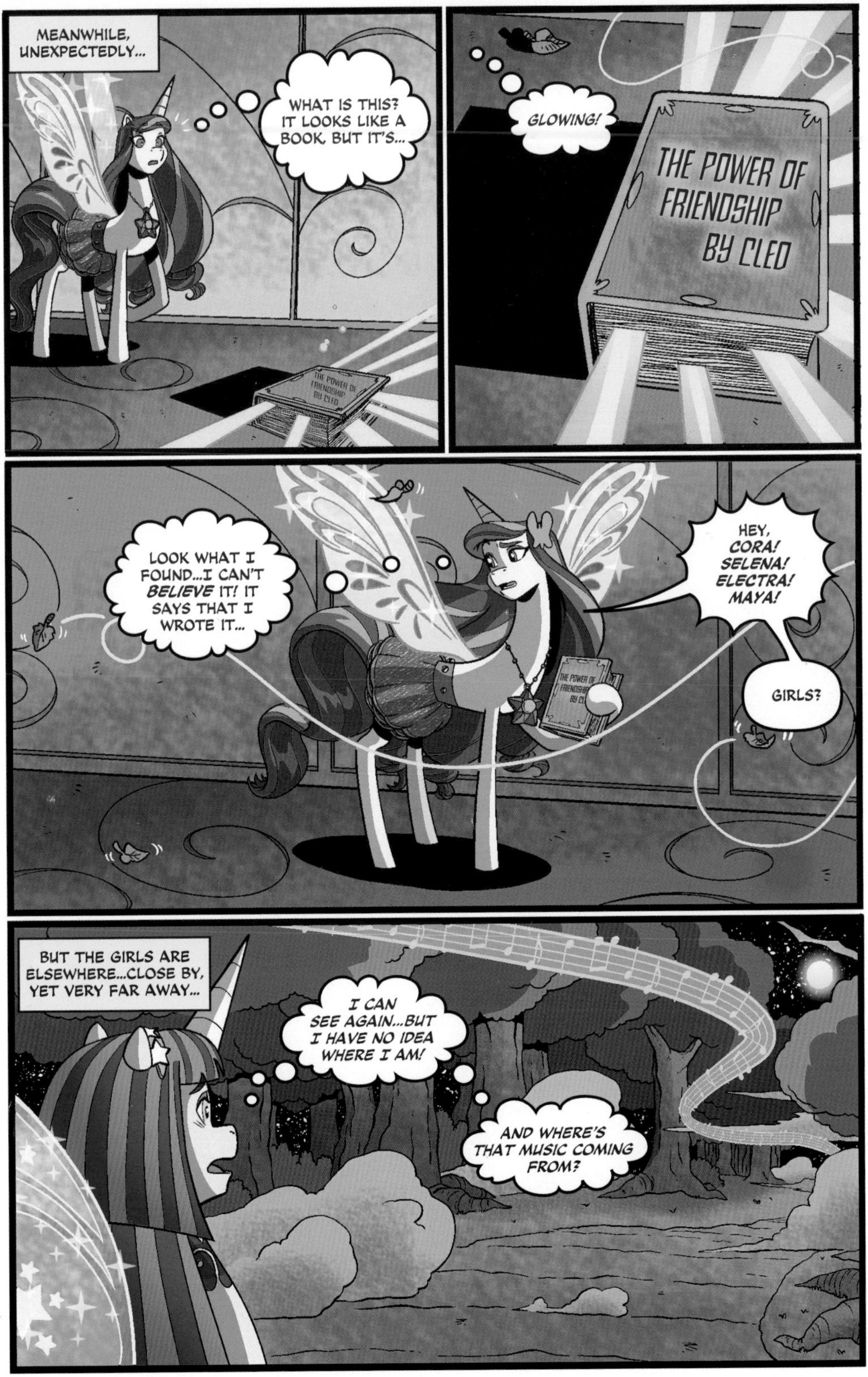
MEANWHILE, UNEXPECTEDLY...
WHAT IS THIS? IT LOOKS LIKE A BOOK, BUT IT'S...
THE POWER OF FRIENDSHIP BY CLEO
GLOWING!
THE POWER OF FRIENDSHIP BY CLEO
LOOK WHAT I FOUND...I CAN'T *BELIEVE* IT! IT SAYS THAT I WROTE IT...
HEY, *CORA! SELENA! ELECTRA! MAYA!*
GIRLS?
BUT THE GIRLS ARE ELSEWHERE...CLOSE BY, YET VERY FAR AWAY...
I CAN SEE AGAIN...BUT I HAVE NO IDEA WHERE I AM!
AND WHERE'S THAT MUSIC COMING FROM?

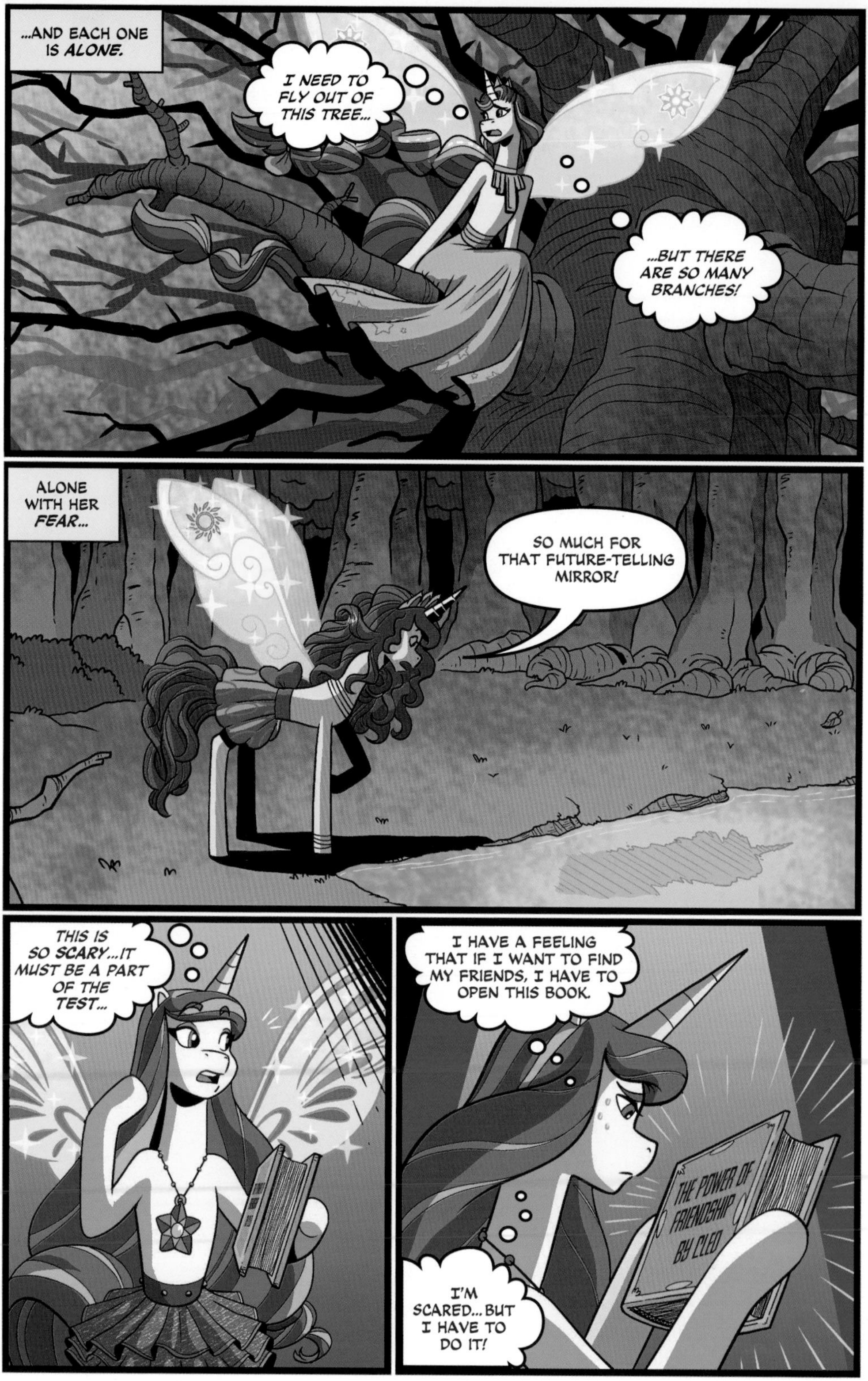
...AND EACH ONE IS ALONE.
I NEED TO FLY OUT OF THIS TREE...
...BUT THERE ARE SO MANY BRANCHES!
ALONE WITH HER FEAR...
SO MUCH FOR THAT FUTURE-TELLING MIRROR!
THIS IS SO SCARY...IT MUST BE A PART OF THE TEST...
I HAVE A FEELING THAT IF I WANT TO FIND MY FRIENDS, I HAVE TO OPEN THIS BOOK.
THE POWER OF FRIENDSHIP BY CLEO
I'M SCARED... BUT I HAVE TO DO IT!

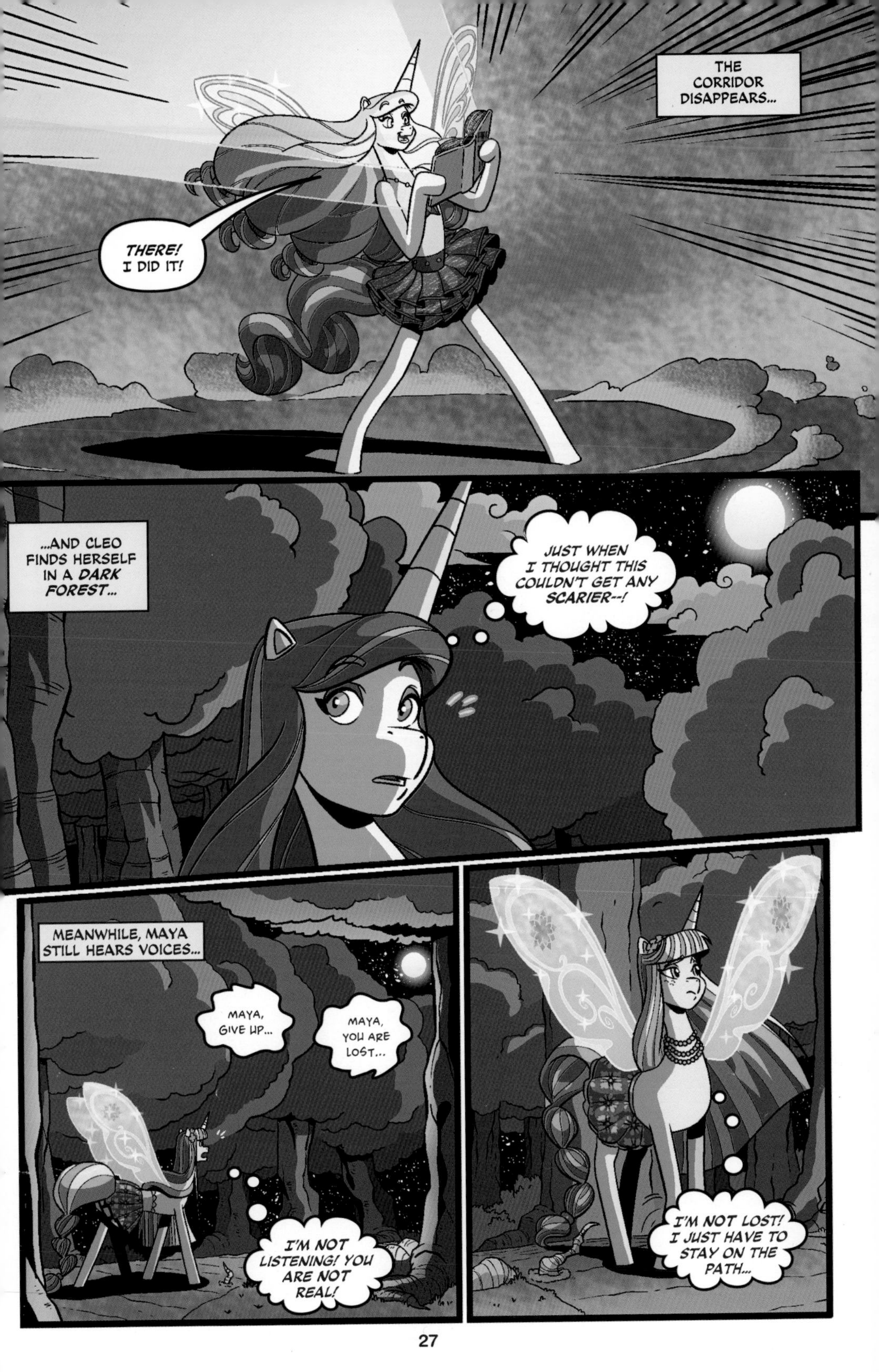
THE CORRIDOR DISAPPEARS...
THERE! I DID IT!
...AND CLEO FINDS HERSELF IN A DARK FOREST...
JUST WHEN I THOUGHT THIS COULDN'T GET ANY SCARIER--!
MEANWHILE, MAYA STILL HEARS VOICES...
MAYA, GIVE UP...
MAYA, YOU ARE LOST...
I'M NOT LISTENING! YOU ARE NOT REAL!
I'M NOT LOST! I JUST HAVE TO STAY ON THE PATH...

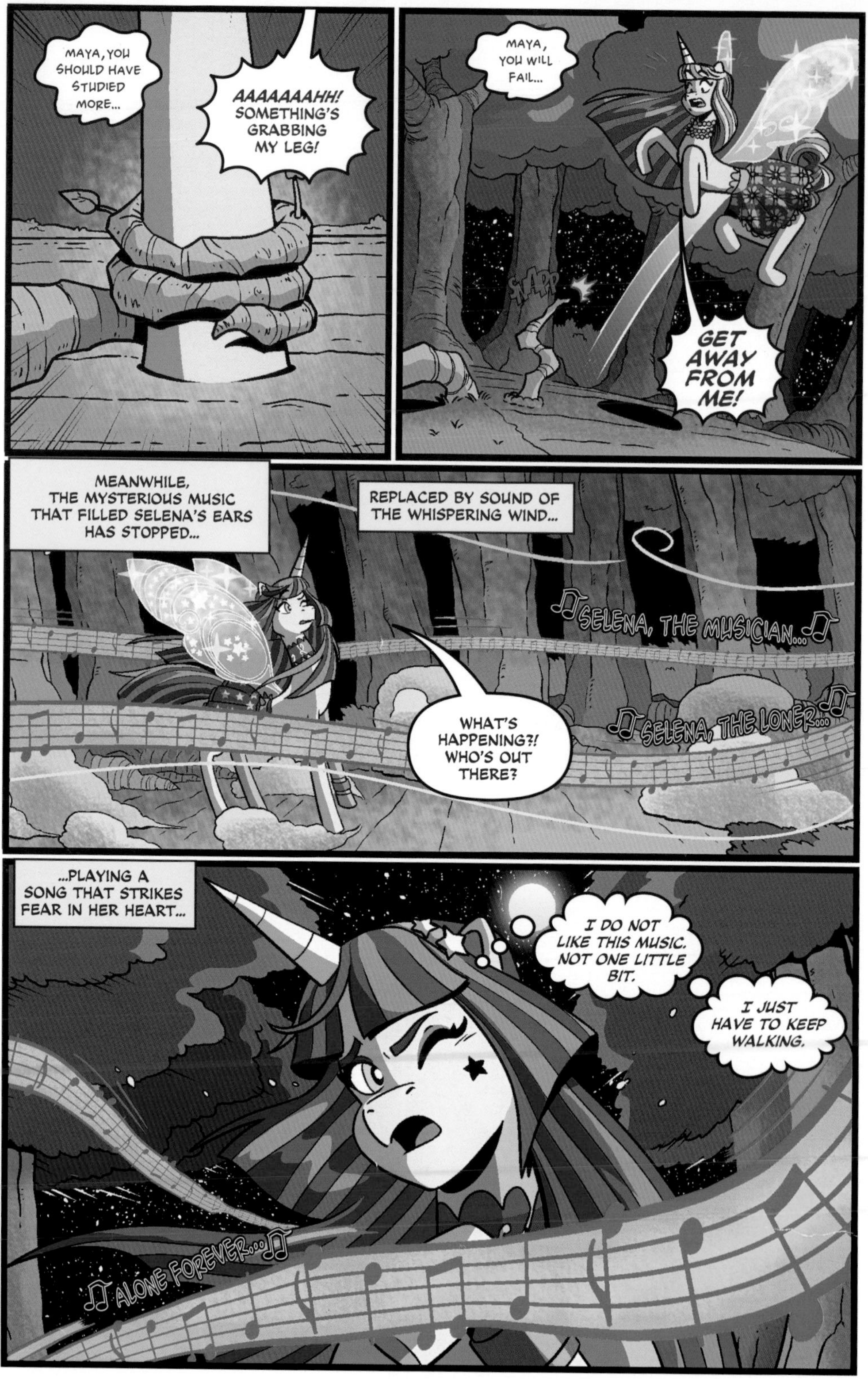
MAYA, YOU SHOULD HAVE STUDIED MORE...
AAAAAAAHH! SOMETHING'S GRABBING MY LEG!
MAYA, YOU WILL FAIL...
SNAPP
GET AWAY FROM ME!
MEANWHILE, THE MYSTERIOUS MUSIC THAT FILLED SELENA'S EARS HAS STOPPED...
REPLACED BY SOUND OF THE WHISPERING WIND...
♫SELENA, THE MUSICIAN...♫
WHAT'S HAPPENING?! WHO'S OUT THERE?
♫SELENA, THE LONER...♫
...PLAYING A SONG THAT STRIKES FEAR IN HER HEART...
I DO NOT LIKE THIS MUSIC. NOT ONE LITTLE BIT.
I JUST HAVE TO KEEP WALKING.
♫ALONE FOREVER...♫

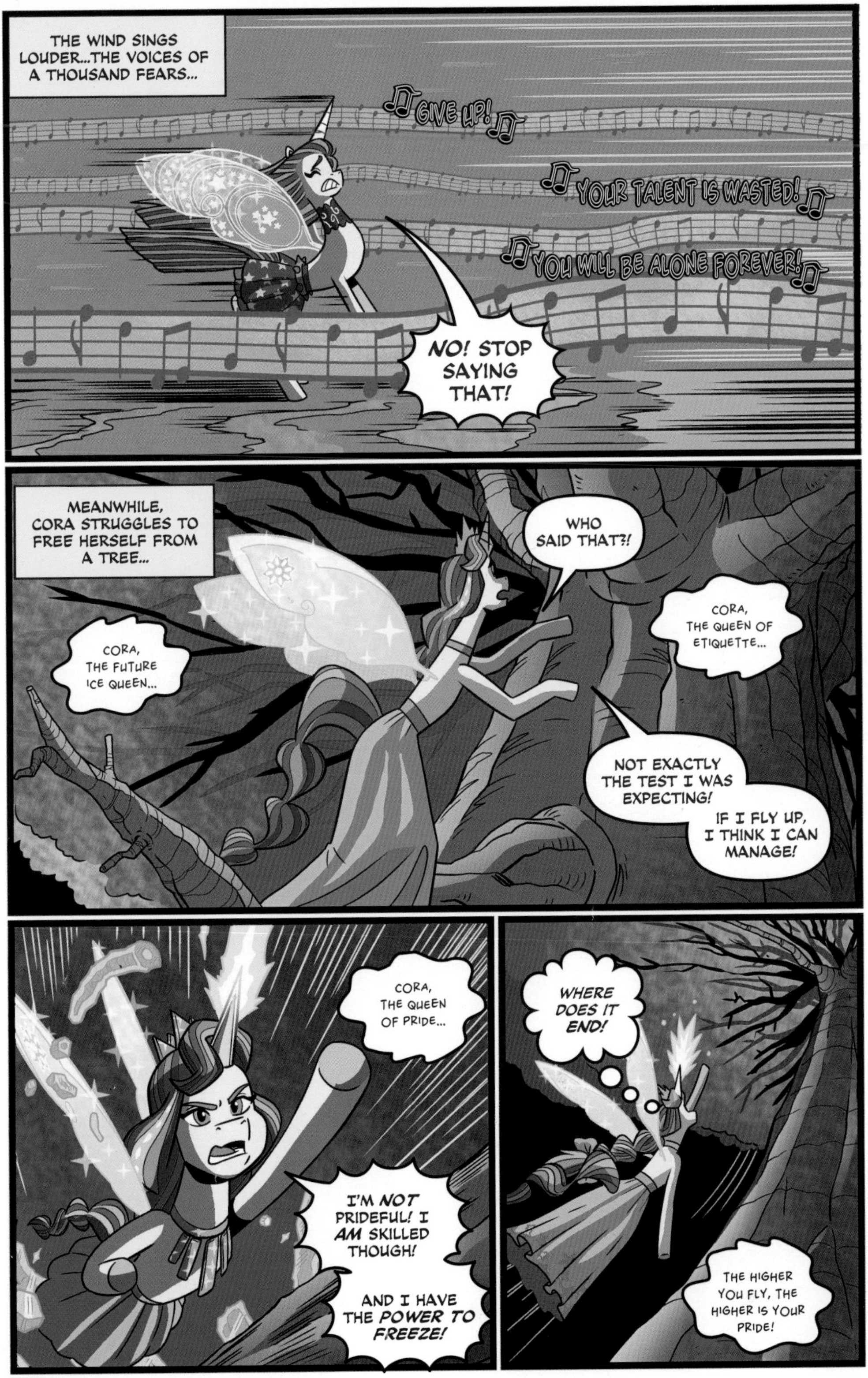
THE WIND SINGS LOUDER...THE VOICES OF A THOUSAND FEARS...
GIVE UP!
YOUR TALENT IS WASTED!
YOU WILL BE ALONE FOREVER!
NO! STOP SAYING THAT!
MEANWHILE, CORA STRUGGLES TO FREE HERSELF FROM A TREE...
WHO SAID THAT?!
CORA, THE FUTURE ICE QUEEN...
CORA, THE QUEEN OF ETIQUETTE...
NOT EXACTLY THE TEST I WAS EXPECTING!
IF I FLY UP, I THINK I CAN MANAGE!
CORA, THE QUEEN OF PRIDE...
I'M NOT PRIDEFUL! I AM SKILLED THOUGH!
AND I HAVE THE POWER TO FREEZE!
WHERE DOES IT END!
THE HIGHER YOU FLY, THE HIGHER IS YOUR PRIDE!

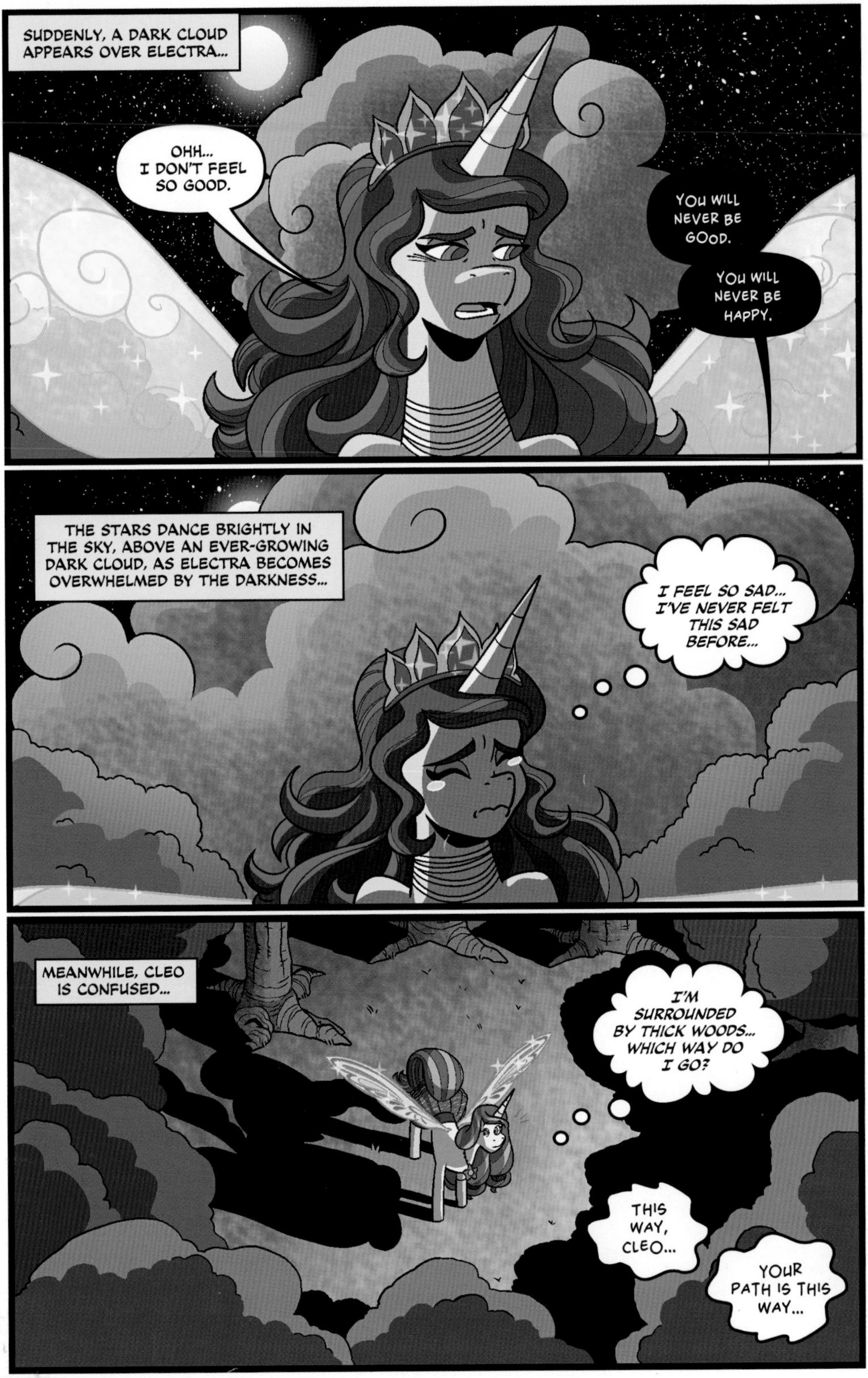
SUDDENLY, A DARK CLOUD APPEARS OVER ELECTRA...
OHH... I DON'T FEEL SO GOOD.
YOU WILL NEVER BE GOOD.
YOU WILL NEVER BE HAPPY.
THE STARS DANCE BRIGHTLY IN THE SKY, ABOVE AN EVER-GROWING DARK CLOUD, AS ELECTRA BECOMES OVERWHELMED BY THE DARKNESS...
I FEEL SO SAD... I'VE NEVER FELT THIS SAD BEFORE...
MEANWHILE, CLEO IS CONFUSED...
I'M SURROUNDED BY THICK WOODS... WHICH WAY DO I GO?
THIS WAY, CLEO...
YOUR PATH IS THIS WAY...

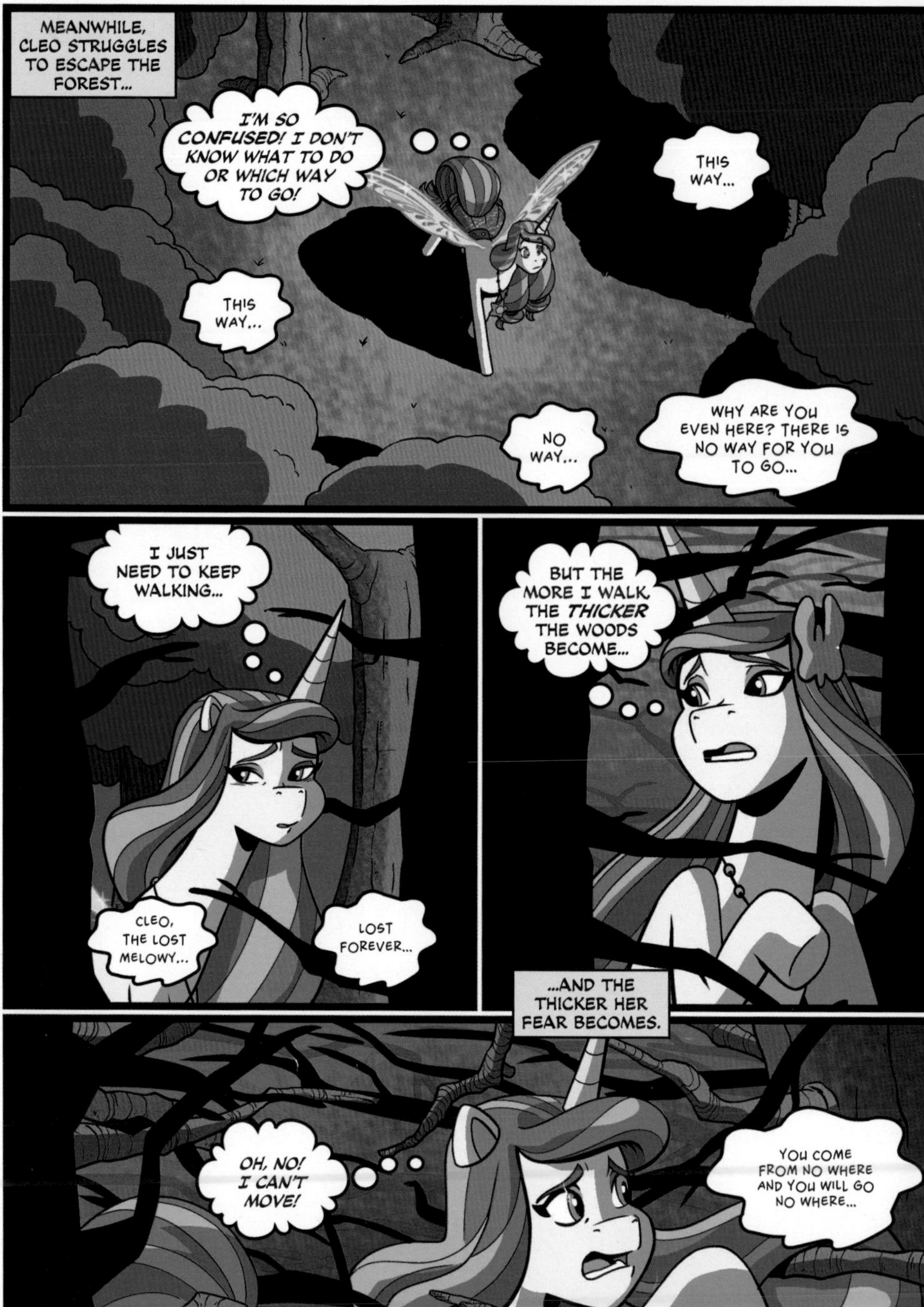
MEANWHILE, CLEO STRUGGLES TO ESCAPE THE FOREST...
I'M SO CONFUSED! I DON'T KNOW WHAT TO DO OR WHICH WAY TO GO!
THIS WAY...
THIS WAY...
NO WAY...
WHY ARE YOU EVEN HERE? THERE IS NO WAY FOR YOU TO GO...
I JUST NEED TO KEEP WALKING...
CLEO, THE LOST MELOWY...
LOST FOREVER...
BUT THE MORE I WALK, THE THICKER THE WOODS BECOME...
...AND THE THICKER HER FEAR BECOMES.
OH, NO! I CAN'T MOVE!
YOU COME FROM NO WHERE AND YOU WILL GO NO WHERE...
THERE IS NO PLACE FOR YOU...

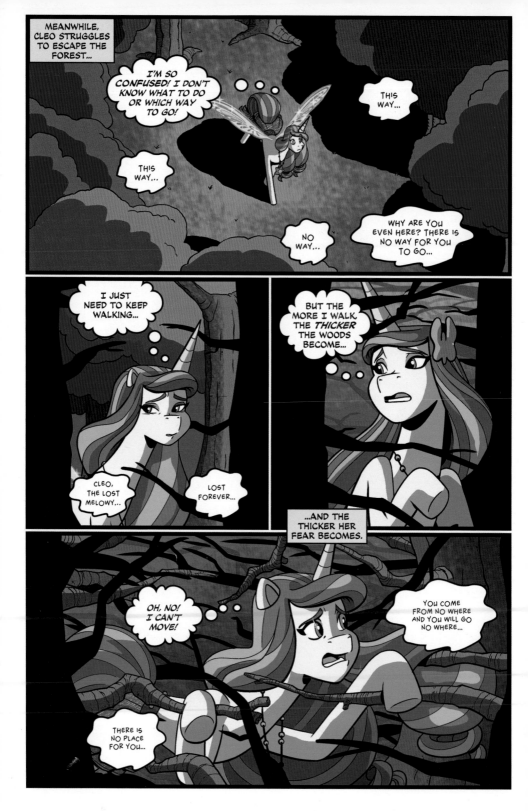

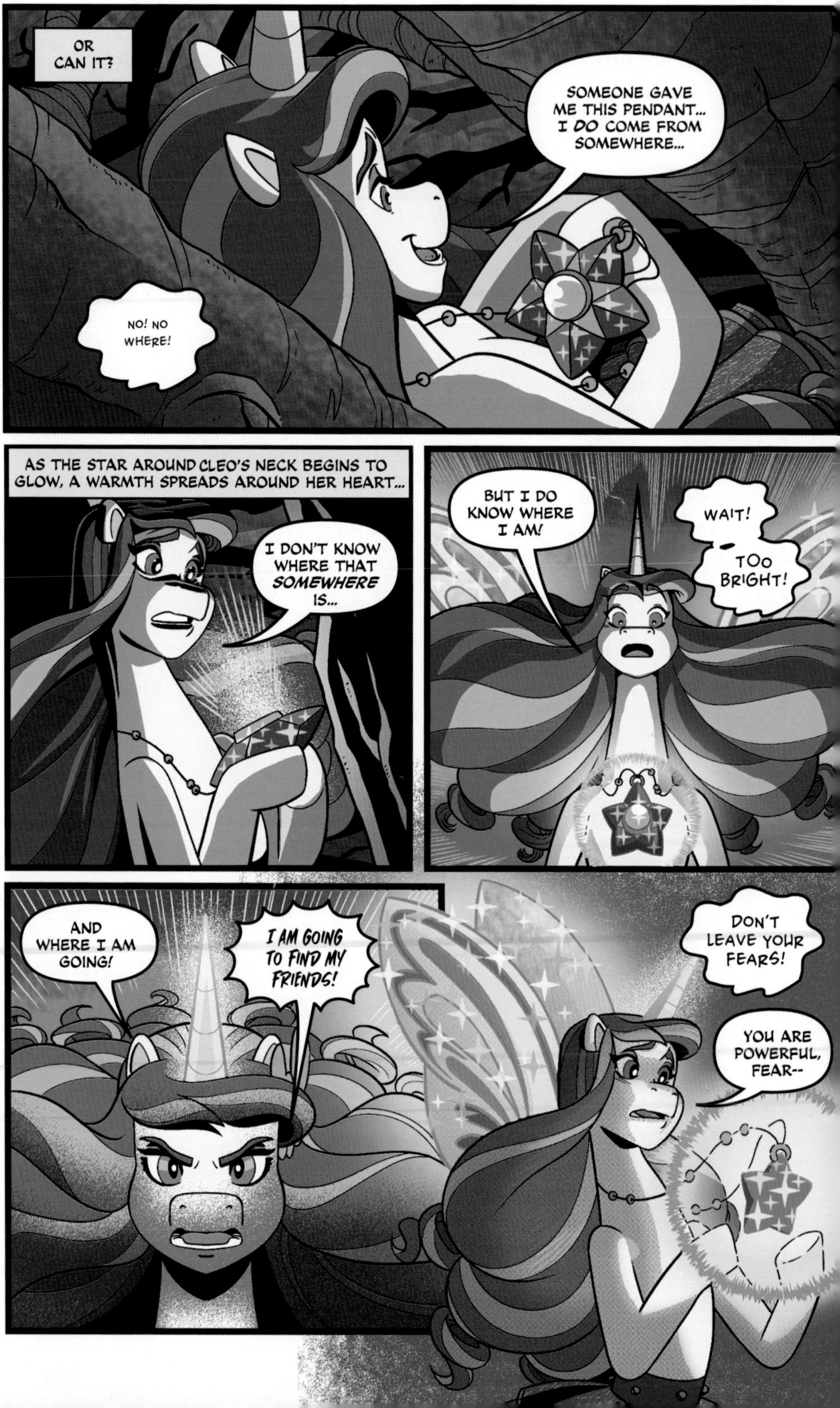
OR CAN IT?
SOMEONE GAVE ME THIS PENDANT... I *DO* COME FROM SOMEWHERE...
NO! NO WHERE!
AS THE STAR AROUND CLEO'S NECK BEGINS TO GLOW, A WARMTH SPREADS AROUND HER HEART...
I DON'T KNOW WHERE THAT *SOMEWHERE* IS...
BUT I DO KNOW WHERE I AM!
WAIT!
TOO BRIGHT!
AND WHERE I AM GOING!
I AM GOING TO FIND MY FRIENDS!
DON'T LEAVE YOUR FEARS!
YOU ARE POWERFUL, FEAR--

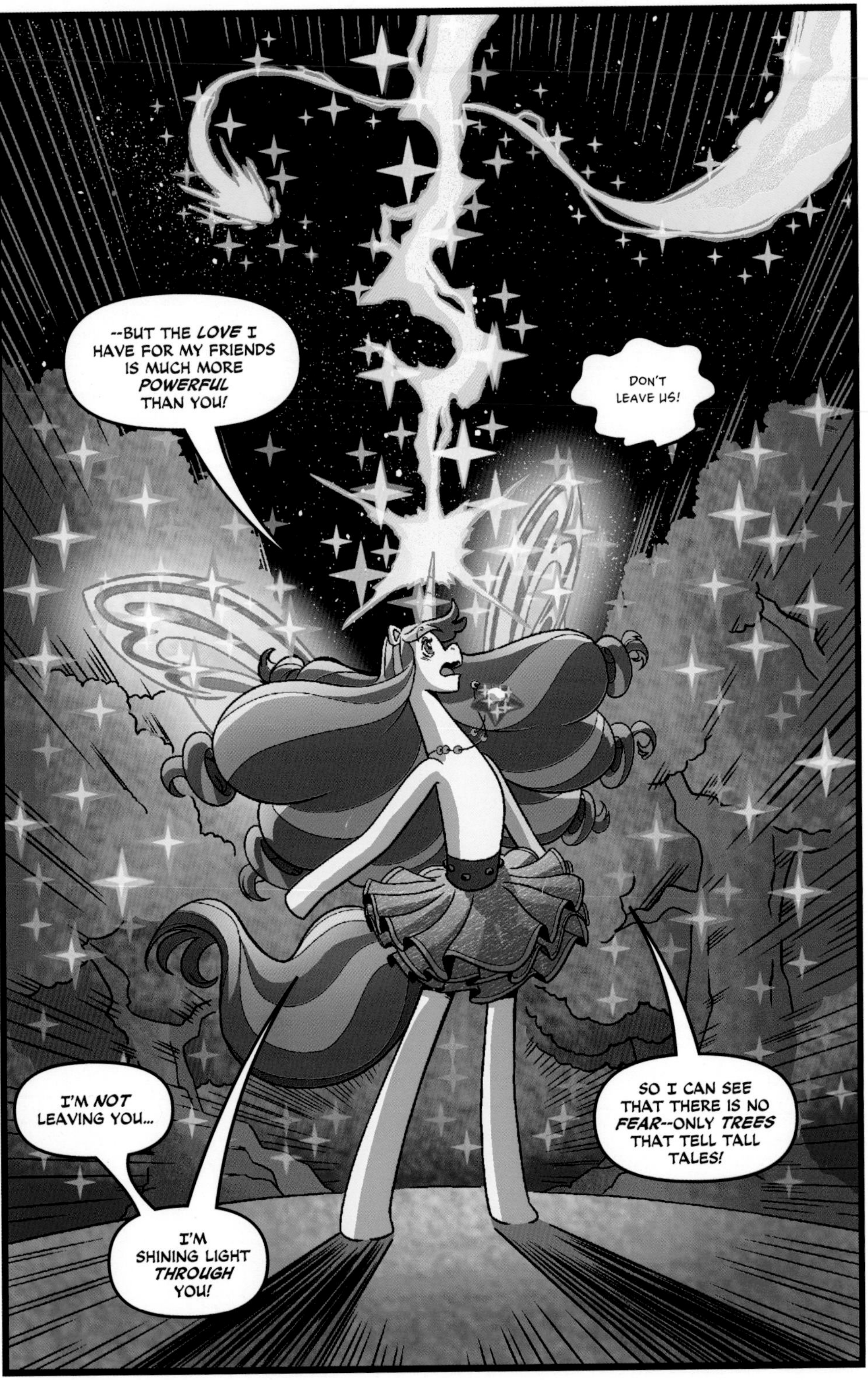
--BUT THE *LOVE* I HAVE FOR MY FRIENDS IS MUCH MORE *POWERFUL* THAN YOU!
DON'T LEAVE US!
I'M *NOT* LEAVING YOU...
I'M SHINING LIGHT *THROUGH* YOU!
SO I CAN SEE THAT THERE IS NO *FEAR*--ONLY *TREES* THAT TELL TALL TALES!

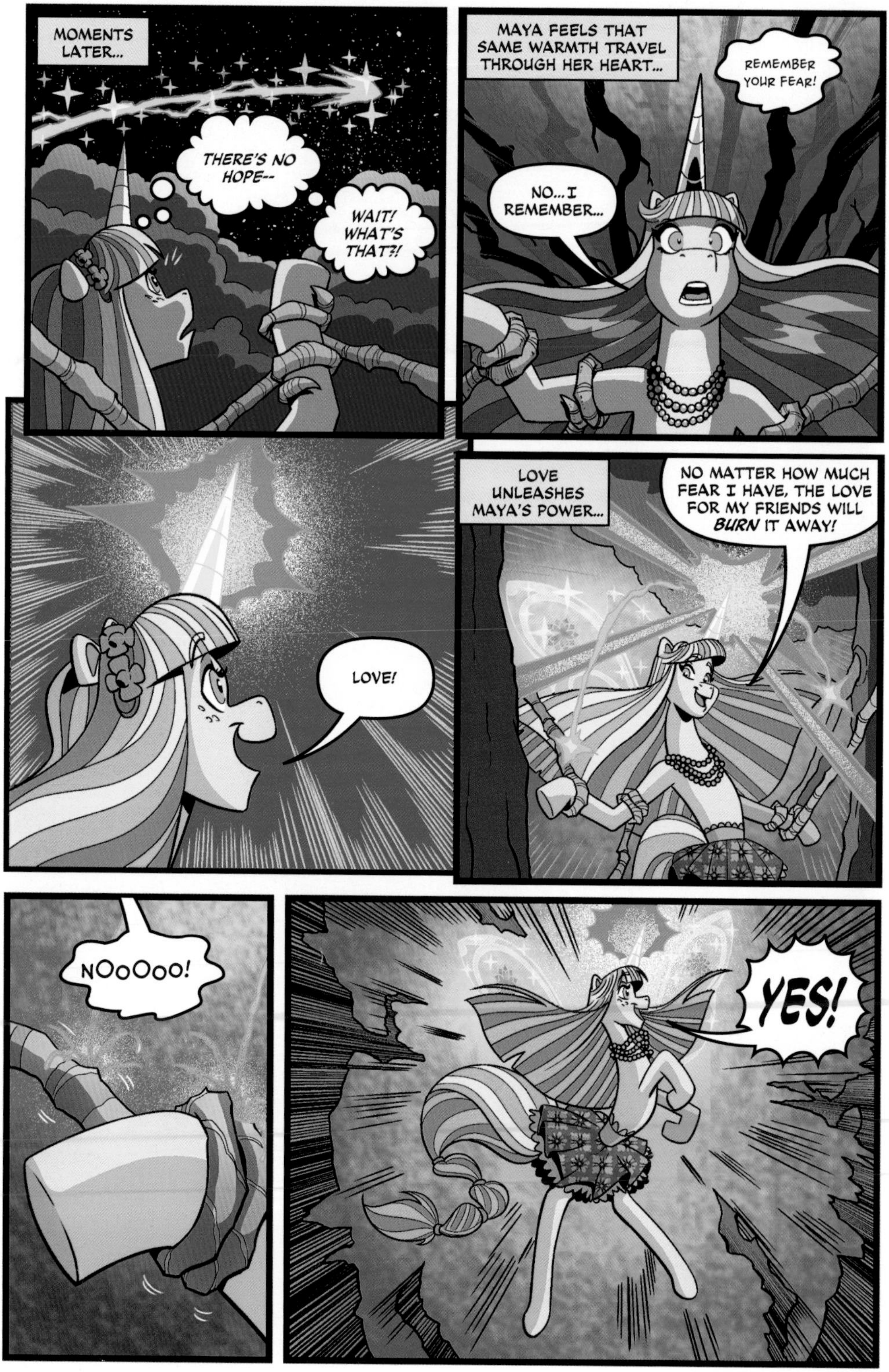
MOMENTS LATER...
THERE'S NO HOPE--
WAIT! WHAT'S THAT?!
MAYA FEELS THAT SAME WARMTH TRAVEL THROUGH HER HEART...
REMEMBER YOUR FEAR!
NO... I REMEMBER...
LOVE!
LOVE UNLEASHES MAYA'S POWER...
NO MATTER HOW MUCH FEAR I HAVE, THE LOVE FOR MY FRIENDS WILL BURN IT AWAY!
NOOOOOO!
YES!

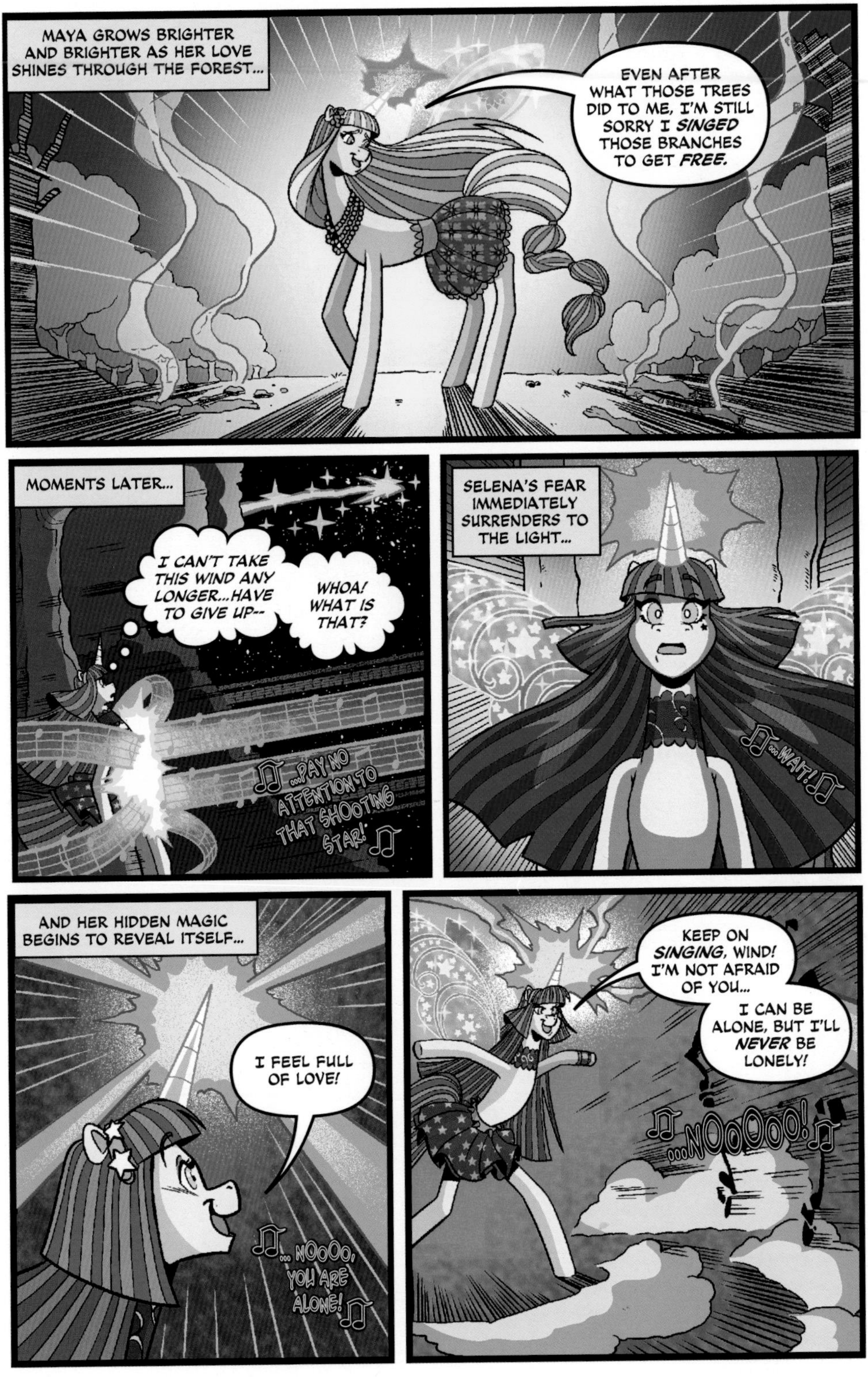
MAYA GROWS BRIGHTER AND BRIGHTER AS HER LOVE SHINES THROUGH THE FOREST...
EVEN AFTER WHAT THOSE TREES DID TO ME, I'M STILL SORRY I SINGED THOSE BRANCHES TO GET FREE.
MOMENTS LATER...
I CAN'T TAKE THIS WIND ANY LONGER...HAVE TO GIVE UP--
WHOA! WHAT IS THAT?
...PAY NO ATTENTION TO THAT SHOOTING STAR!
SELENA'S FEAR IMMEDIATELY SURRENDERS TO THE LIGHT...
...WAIT!
AND HER HIDDEN MAGIC BEGINS TO REVEAL ITSELF...
I FEEL FULL OF LOVE!
... NOOOO, YOU ARE ALONE!
KEEP ON SINGING, WIND! I'M NOT AFRAID OF YOU...
I CAN BE ALONE, BUT I'LL NEVER BE LONELY!
...NOOOOO!

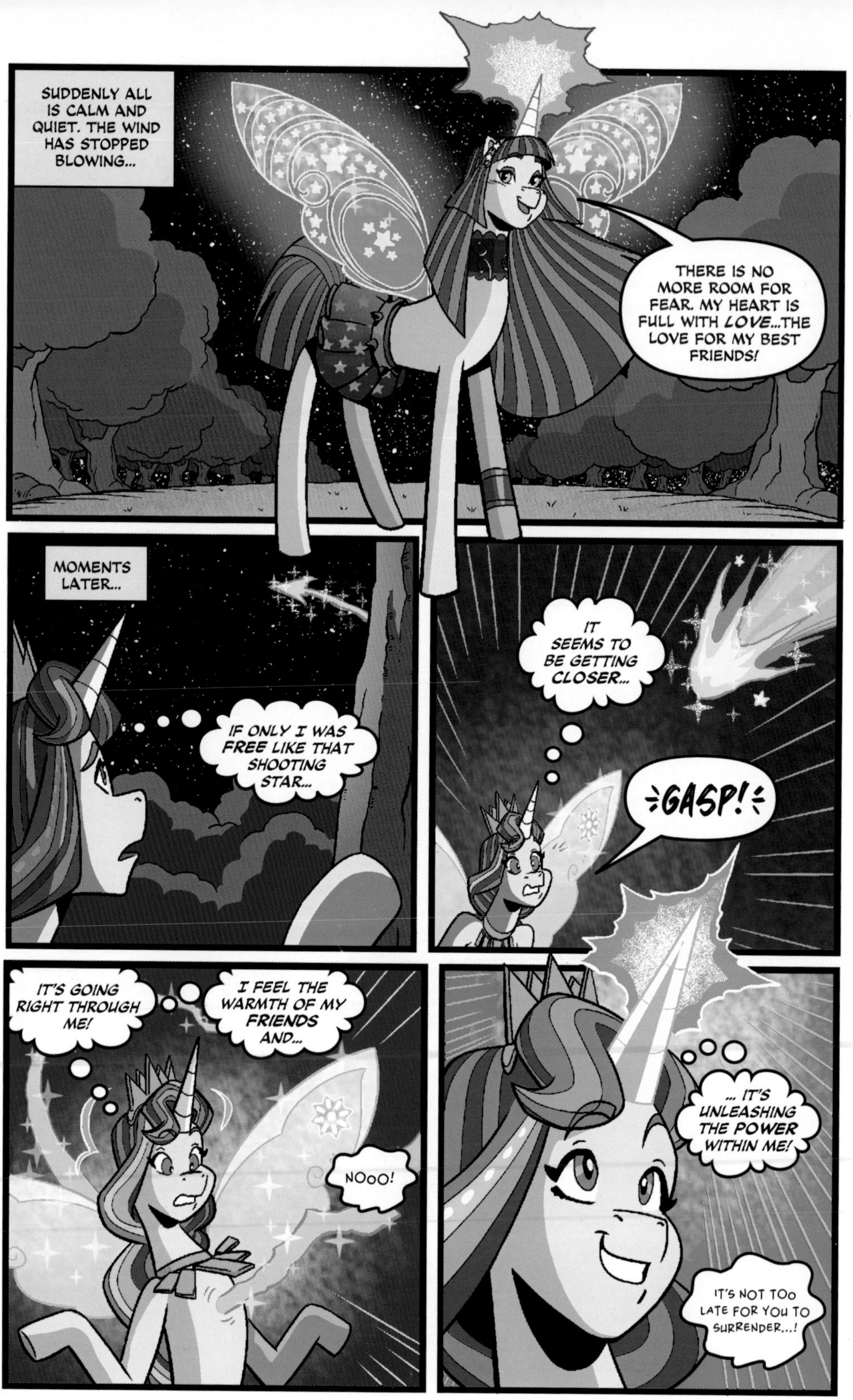

SUDDENLY ALL IS CALM AND QUIET. THE WIND HAS STOPPED BLOWING...
THERE IS NO MORE ROOM FOR FEAR. MY HEART IS FULL WITH *LOVE*...THE LOVE FOR MY BEST FRIENDS!
MOMENTS LATER...
IF ONLY I WAS FREE LIKE THAT SHOOTING STAR...
IT SEEMS TO BE GETTING CLOSER...
GASP!
IT'S GOING RIGHT THROUGH ME!
I FEEL THE WARMTH OF MY FRIENDS AND...
NOoO!
... IT'S UNLEASHING THE POWER WITHIN ME!
IT'S NOT TOo LATE FOR YOU TO SURRENDER...!

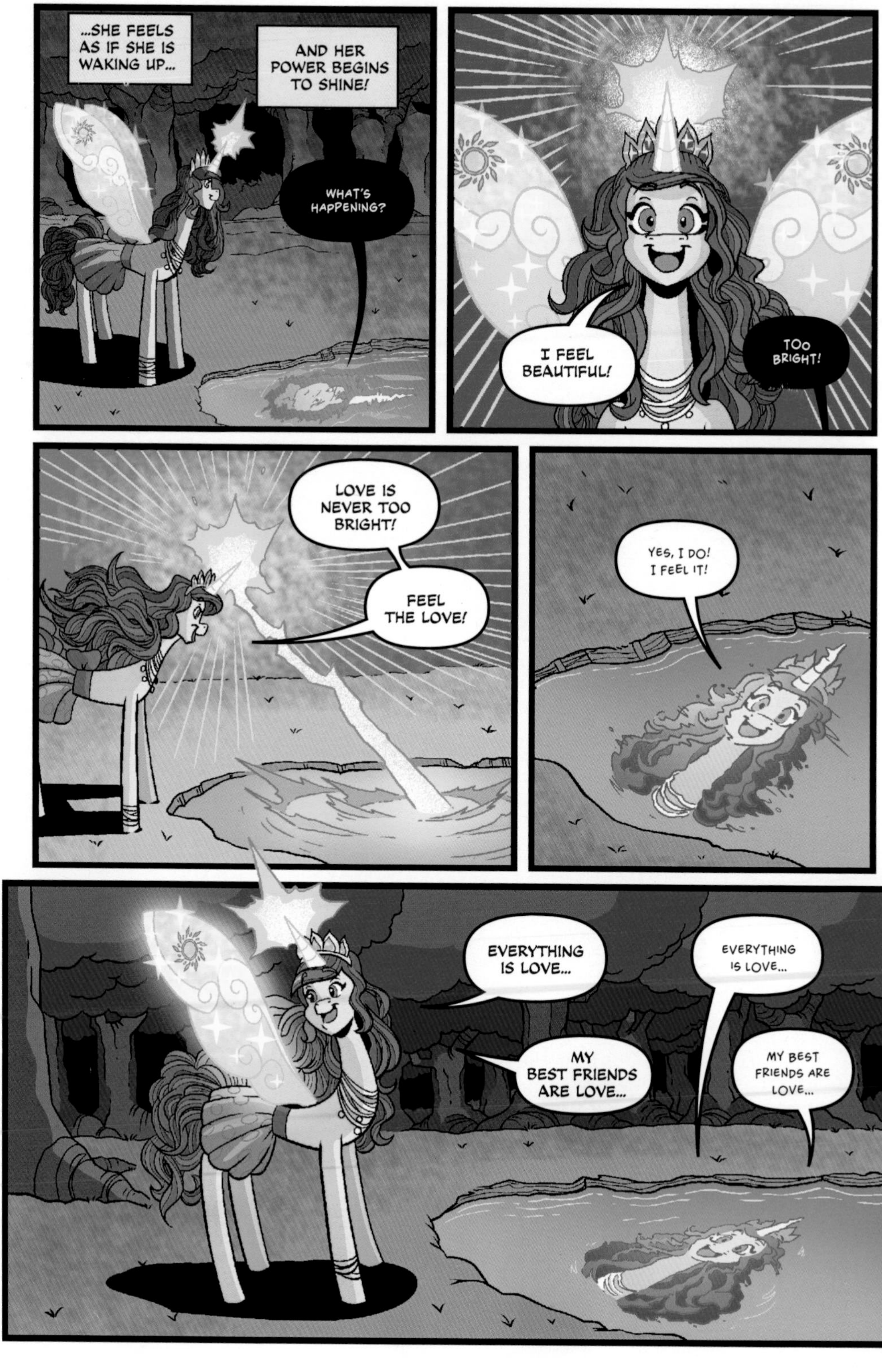

...SHE FEELS AS IF SHE IS WAKING UP...
AND HER POWER BEGINS TO SHINE!
WHAT'S HAPPENING?
I FEEL BEAUTIFUL!
TOo BRIGHT!
LOVE IS NEVER TOO BRIGHT!
FEEL THE LOVE!
YES, I DO! I FEEL IT!
EVERYTHING IS LOVE...
EVERYTHING IS LOVE...
MY BEST FRIENDS ARE LOVE...
MY BEST FRIENDS ARE LOVE...

43

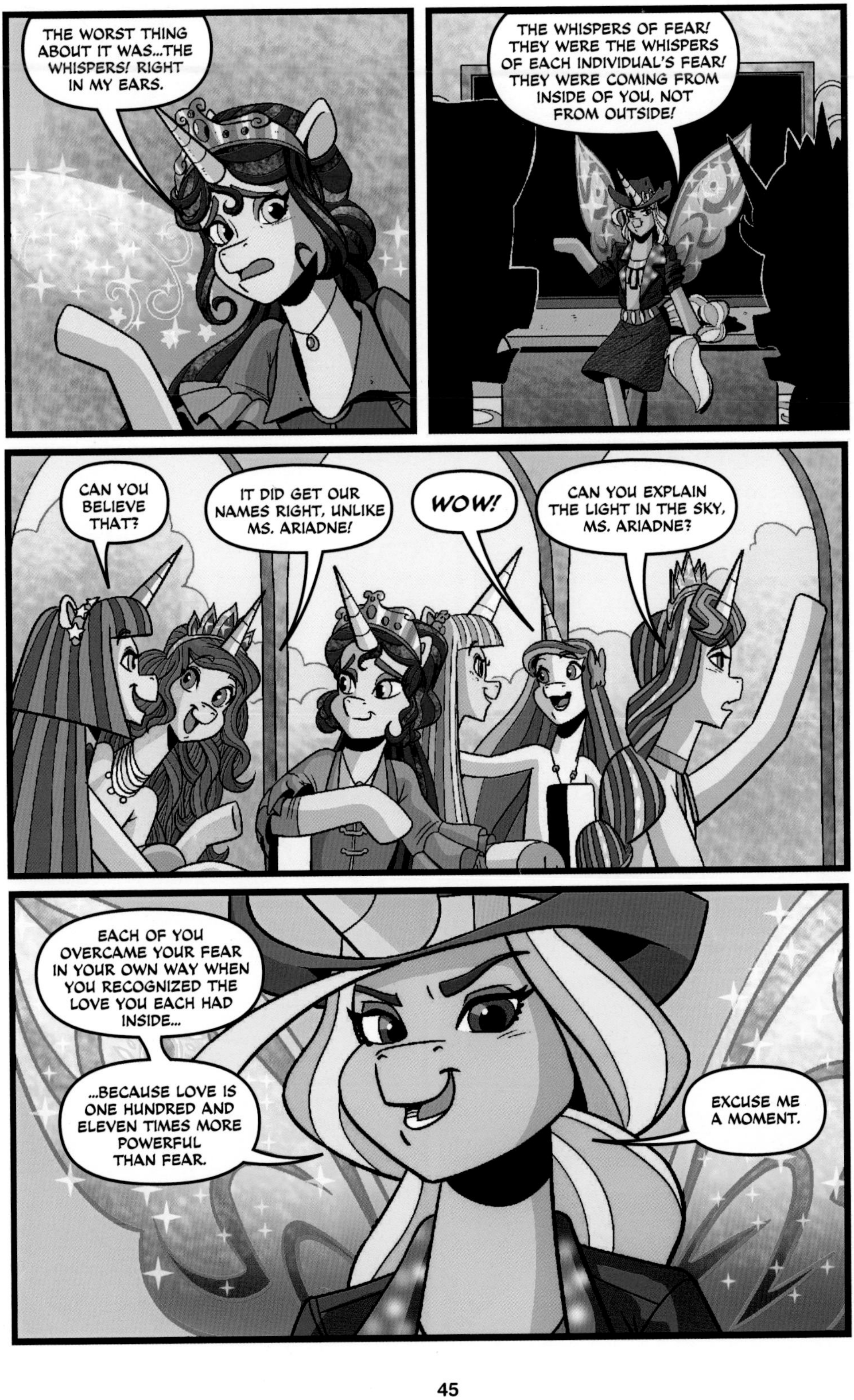
THE WORST THING ABOUT IT WAS...THE WHISPERS! RIGHT IN MY EARS.
THE WHISPERS OF FEAR! THEY WERE THE WHISPERS OF EACH INDIVIDUAL'S FEAR! THEY WERE COMING FROM INSIDE OF YOU, NOT FROM OUTSIDE!
CAN YOU BELIEVE THAT?
IT DID GET OUR NAMES RIGHT, UNLIKE MS. ARIADNE!
WOW!
CAN YOU EXPLAIN THE LIGHT IN THE SKY, MS. ARIADNE?
EACH OF YOU OVERCAME YOUR FEAR IN YOUR OWN WAY WHEN YOU RECOGNIZED THE LOVE YOU EACH HAD INSIDE...
...BECAUSE LOVE IS ONE HUNDRED AND ELEVEN TIMES MORE POWERFUL THAN FEAR.
EXCUSE ME A MOMENT.

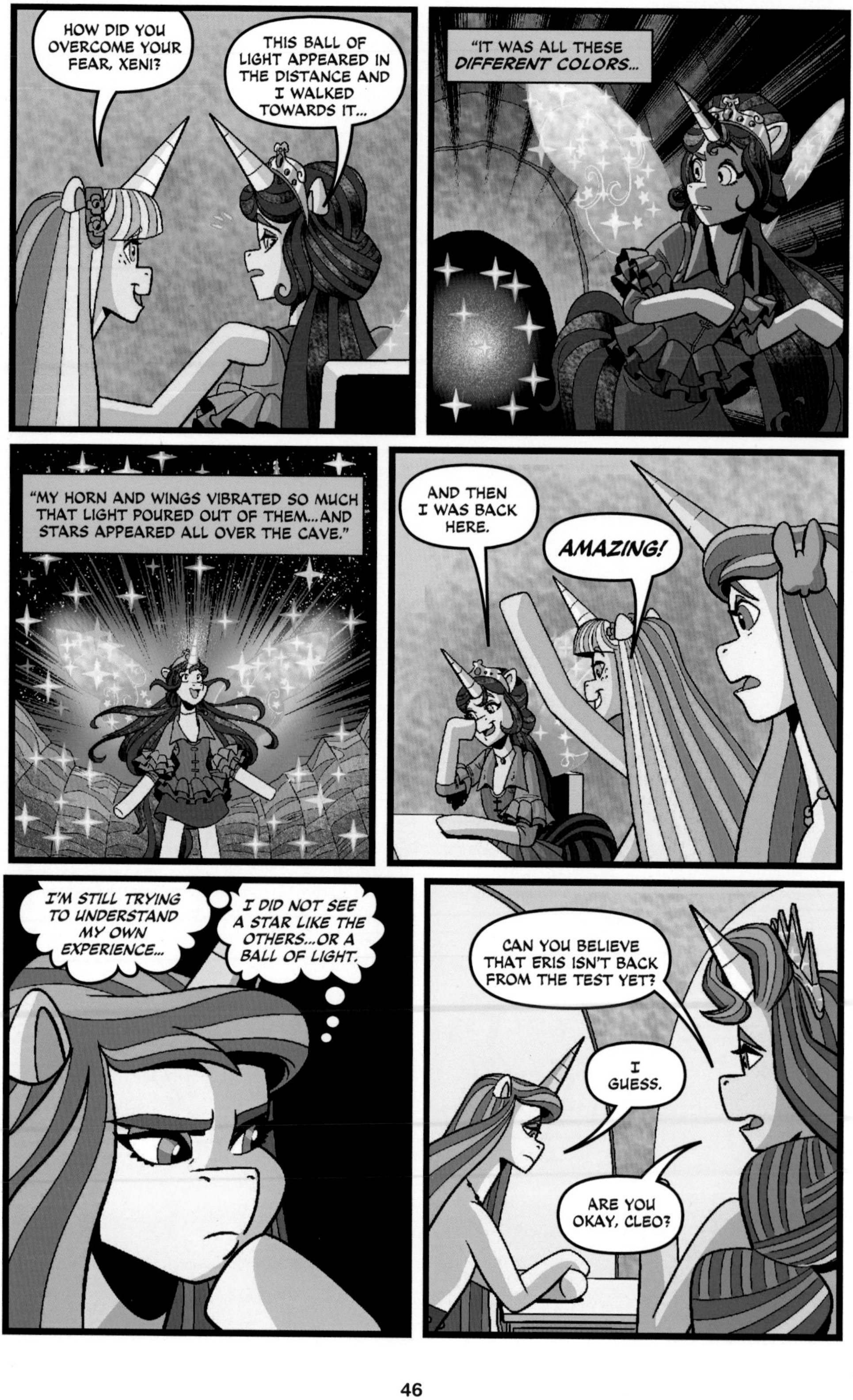
HOW DID YOU OVERCOME YOUR FEAR, XENI?
THIS BALL OF LIGHT APPEARED IN THE DISTANCE AND I WALKED TOWARDS IT...
"IT WAS ALL THESE DIFFERENT COLORS...
"MY HORN AND WINGS VIBRATED SO MUCH THAT LIGHT POURED OUT OF THEM...AND STARS APPEARED ALL OVER THE CAVE."
AND THEN I WAS BACK HERE.
AMAZING!
I'M STILL TRYING TO UNDERSTAND MY OWN EXPERIENCE...
I DID NOT SEE A STAR LIKE THE OTHERS...OR A BALL OF LIGHT.
CAN YOU BELIEVE THAT ERIS ISN'T BACK FROM THE TEST YET?
I GUESS.
ARE YOU OKAY, CLEO?

48

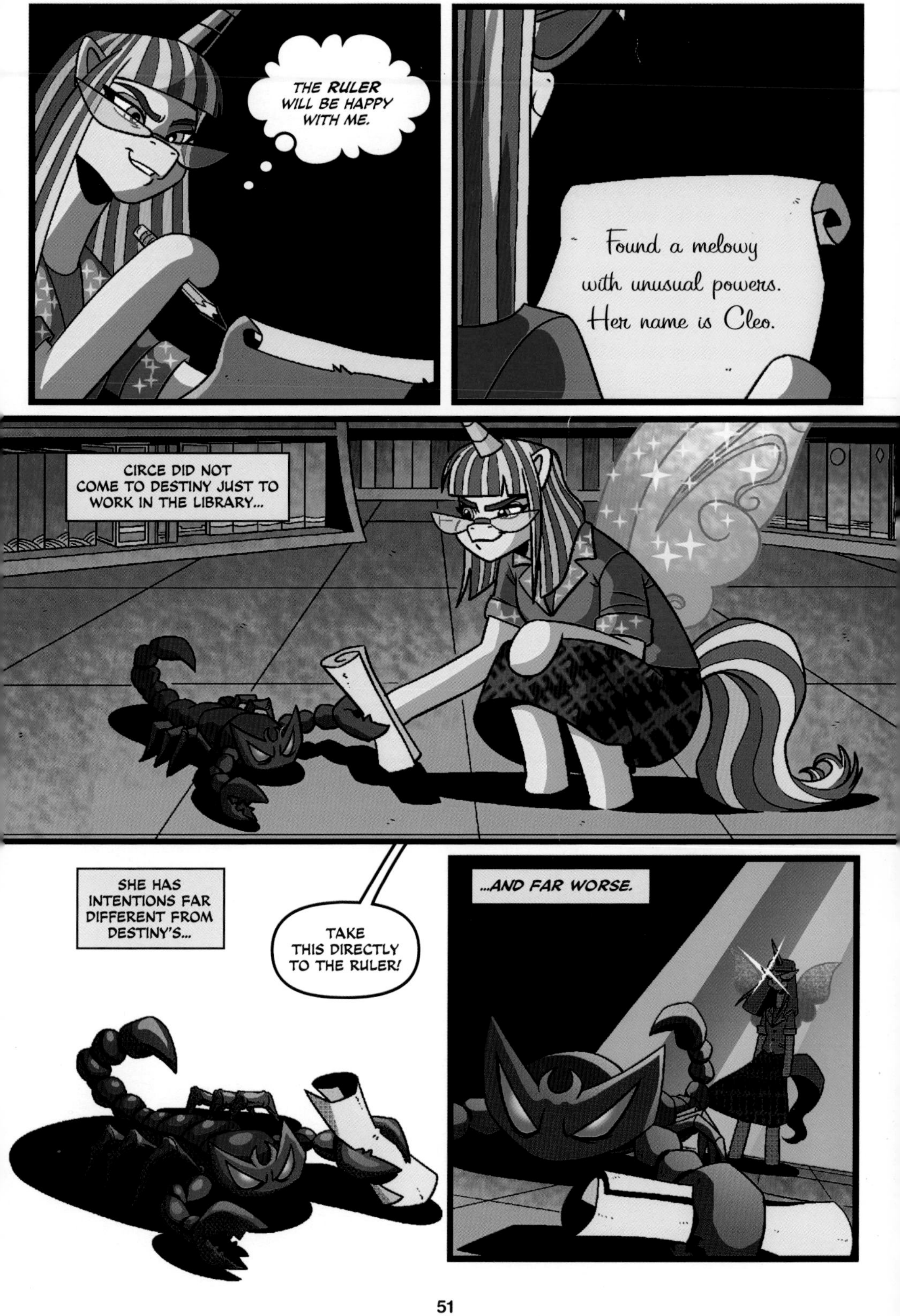
THE RULER WILL BE HAPPY WITH ME.
Found a melowy with unusual powers. Her name is Cleo.
CIRCE DID NOT COME TO DESTINY JUST TO WORK IN THE LIBRARY...
SHE HAS INTENTIONS FAR DIFFERENT FROM DESTINY'S...
TAKE THIS DIRECTLY TO THE RULER!
...AND FAR WORSE.

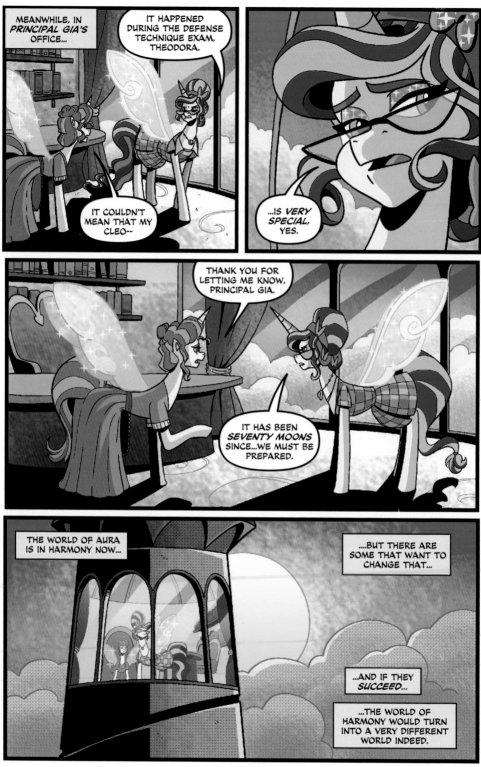

-END-

WATCH OUT FOR PAPERCUTZ™

Welcome to the marvelous and magical premiere MELOWY graphic novel, by Cortney Powell and Ryan Jampole based on the characters created by Danielle Star, from Papercutz, the Pegasus-friendly folks dedicated to publishing graphic novels for all ages. I'm Jim Salicrup, the Editor-in-Chief and part-time hall monitor at Destiny. Generally, within this column, I'll take you behind-the-scenes at Papercutz and let you know what we're cooking up for you next. But before we get to that, let's talk about MELOWY a bit…

People often ask us at Papercutz how do we decide what we're going to publish? Good question! The obvious and most honest answer would be we try to find great characters, in well-written stories, illustrated with beautiful artwork, and we hope it will attract as large an audience as possible. After all, the reality of the publishing business is if you don't sell enough books, then you'll go out of business. We're entering our thirteenth year of publishing graphic novels, so we must be doing something right.

But that doesn't answer the question of why we're now launching MELOWY. The answer may surprise you, because it all started (as a great man once said) with a mouse. Back in 2008, Papercutz started publishing the graphic novel adventures of GERONIMO STILTON. He's the editor of The Rodent's Gazette, the most *famous* newspaper on Mouse Island. Geronimo is often attempting to thwart his arch foes, The Pirate Cats, who have discovered a way to travel back in time and change history. In other words, GERONIMO STILTON is all about saving the future by protecting the past.

The GERONIMO STILTON graphic novels were so popular that we're still publishing them today, and over the years we even published the spin-off series, THEA STILTON, which featured five Mouseford Academy students who were inspired by Geronimo's sister, Thea Stilton, the famous journalist, to become journalists themselves. They even call themselves The Thea Sisters. Both GERONIMO STILTON and THEA STILTON were originally based on an original idea by Elisabetta Dami, and marketed around the world by a company called Atlantyca. We absolutely love working with everyone at Atlantyca, and when they told us about a new project that featured flying unicorns attending a magical school, we knew we had to publish MELOWY graphic novels too!

So here we are, the first MELOWY graphic novel is completed and we couldn't be more excited! We really want to know what you think of Cleo, Electra, Eris, Flora, Selena, and everyone else attending Destiny! See the box below to see how you may contact us to share your thoughts on MELOWY…

Hey, remember we said "it all started with a mouse"? Well, what better way to end this graphic novel than to offer a peek at that mouse's latest offering from Papercutz— GERONIMO STILTON 3 IN 1! It's a special book that features the first three GERONIMO STILTON graphic novels all in just one book! So let's go back to the future and enjoy the opening pages of Geronimo's very first graphic novel, "The Discovery of America." It starts on the very next page!

If all goes well, we'll be back with MELOWY #2 "The Fashion Club of Colors" before you know it! Until then, be sure to visit papercutz.com for the latest news on MELOWY and all our other great graphic novels. And be sure to tell your friends about MELOWY too! Some things are just too wonderful to keep all to yourself!

Thanks,

Jim

STAY IN TOUCH!

EMAIL: salicrup@papercutz.com
WEB: papercutz.com
TWITTER: @papercutzgn

INSTAGRAM: @papercutzgn
FACEBOOK: PAPERCUTZGRAPHICNOVELS
SNAIL MAIL: Papercutz, 160 Broadway, Suite 700, East Wing, New York, NY 10038

Here's a special preview of
GERONIMO STILTON 3 IN 1 #1...

59

*DON'T TALK NONSENSE!

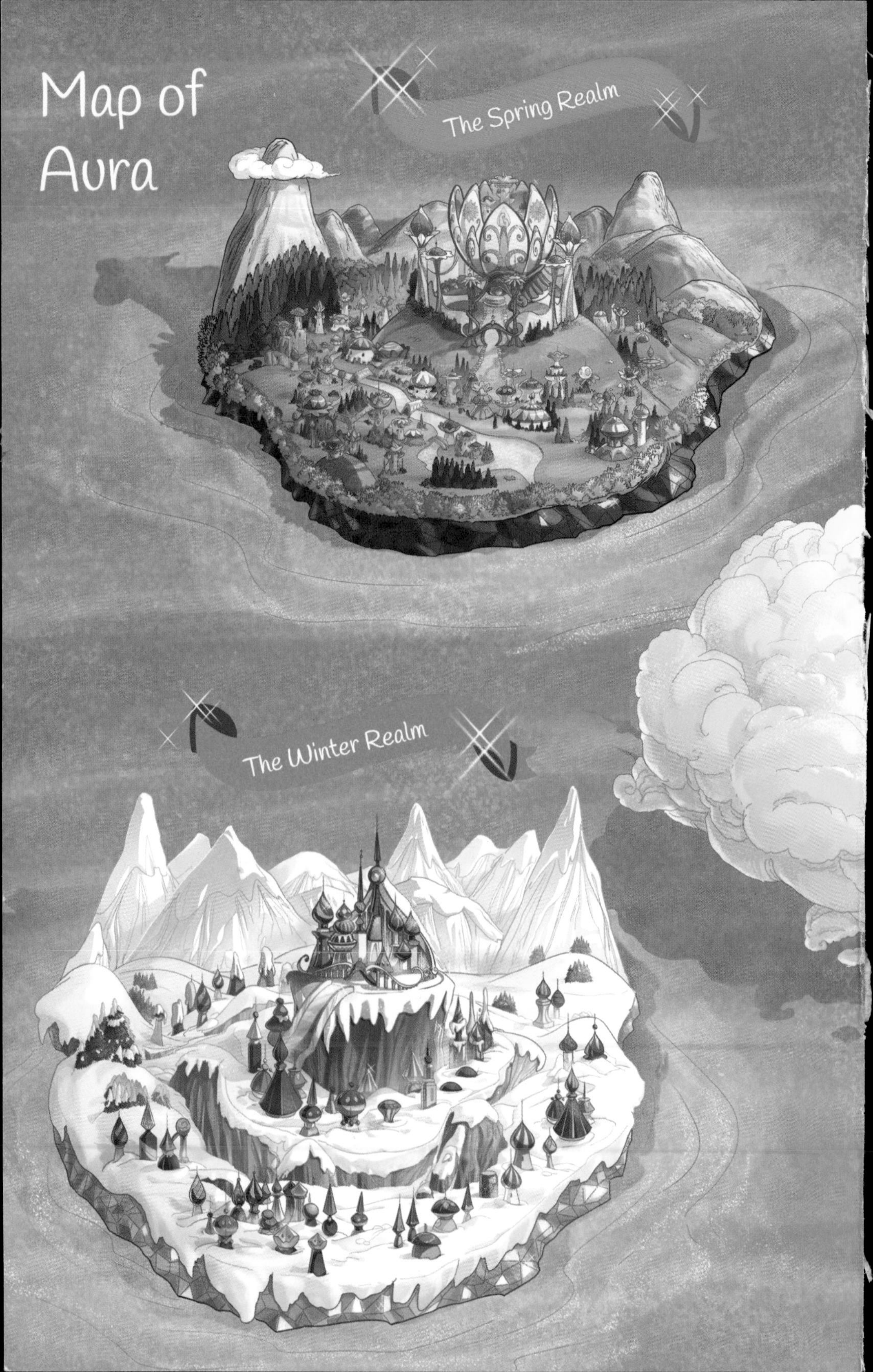
Map of Aura
The Spring Realm
The Winter Realm